At Megan's touch, feelings exploded inside Rafe, feelings he'd thought were dead and gone

He felt Megan's breasts against his side, her hand touching his, her breath fanning his skin and her scent filling him. Shaken and trying to recover, he moved to disentangle himself.

Rafe wanted her in the most basic way. She was a total stranger, a woman who was opinionated and infuriating...and incredibly desirable. A woman who made his whole body ache with need, whose presence warmed his soul.

But being with Megan, no matter how good it would feel, was wrong. He needed to stop thinking of her as anything more than someone he'd just caught rifling through her boss's desk. That was his job. But as she stood and increased some of the space between them, he knew he'd never stop thinking about her. It was impossible.

As impossible as wanting a woman like her...

Dear Reader,

When Megan Smiles is the next story in my JUST FOR KIDS series, and comes with a special heroine. Megan Gallagher has everything in her life in place: a perfect, fast-track career and an equally perfect fiancé. But what she hasn't counted on is meeting a security guard named Rafe, and realizing that there can be totally different versions of a "perfect" life.

Rafe Dagget is a widower with twins who has decided he's loved once and completely. And he continues to believe that until he meets Megan and sees her smile. Both Megan and Rafe are in for big surprises in this story—life-changing surprises. And there's a surprise for you, too, at the end of the book, which I hope proves it's never too late to find that one special person in this life, and to truly fall in love...again.

WHEN MEGAN SMILES

Mary Anne Wilson

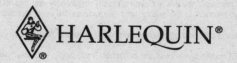

HARLEQUIN®

TORONTO • NEW YORK • LONDON
AMSTERDAM • PARIS • SYDNEY • HAMBURG
STOCKHOLM • ATHENS • TOKYO • MILAN • MADRID
PRAGUE • WARSAW • BUDAPEST • AUCKLAND

ISBN 0-373-75013-7

WHEN MEGAN SMILES

Visit us at www.eHarlequin.com

Printed in U.S.A.

For Beulah Wilson
A great mother-in-law and an even better friend.
Thanks for being part of my life.

Prologue

Rafe Dagget looked at the "perfect" woman across the table from him at one of the best and most intimate restaurants in the city. He wasn't so sure she was perfect, or even close. But Dave Lang, his friend who had talked him into this blind date, had been adamant.

"She's pretty, smart, and she loves kids. She's perfect, Rafe, just perfect."

Rafe had tried to get out of the date, but Dave hadn't given him a chance. "We all loved Gabriella, you know that, and there won't be another woman like her, Rafe." Dave's slightly florid face had gone from intently concerned to being touched by a sad but knowing smile. "But, buddy, it's time. It's been two years. You need to get out and meet people. You have to move on with your life, for your sake and the sake of the twins."

Rafe watched the woman talking to him, and part of him reluctantly agreed with Dave's assessment. His blind date was pretty, in a girlish sort of way, with an upturned nose, dark eyes, full lips and red hair cut into a stylish feathery cap. But perfect? He doubted that. As much as he doubted Dave's pronouncement that it was "time to move on." Why did everyone believe that two years was the magic amount of time to get over a death that left rubble behind and a gaping hole in a life?

"I always thought four children would be perfect," his blind date was saying earnestly, leaning toward him across the table, making intent eye contact with him. "Just perfect."

Rafe reached for his wineglass, breaking the contact when he realized how freely people tossed around the word *perfect*. On top of that, he couldn't remember the woman's name. Felicia, Fanny? He swallowed a good half of the smooth merlot before he put the goblet back down on the white linen cloth.

"Two boys, two girls," she rattled. "Two years apart."

"Hmm," he murmured, because he was thinking that the restaurant, with its dim lights and soft mood music, suddenly seemed claustrophobic. He'd been here before, in another life when the world had been right. Then it might have been perfect.

He drained the rest of his wine as his nameless date leaned closer to him across the table. Now he didn't know what she'd been saying and tried to pick up the threads of her conversation. She tapped her bare wrist. "And my biological clock is ticking. If I want to have children, I need to get started. Francine, I said to myself a few weeks ago, you're thirty years old, and you'd better get on with things.''

Francine. That was it. And Francine was dead serious about what she was saying. ''Absolutely,'' he said, buying time while he tried to figure out how to end this date as quickly as possible.

''Absolutely,'' she echoed with an emphatic shake of her head. ''As soon as I know that I'm having a child, I'm going to apply at the Briar School. Fantastic school. Do you know they vet everyone who applies? Quite hard to get your child into it.''

Rafe casually glanced at his watch. They'd been at the restaurant for only half an hour, but it seemed like a lifetime. ''A good school is important,'' he murmured, just to say something.

She grinned a toothy smile, as if she'd won a jackpot, and reached over to tap the back of his hand that held the wine goblet. ''From what David told me about you, I knew you'd understand, that we'd be on the same page.''

Understand what, and what page? Then she answered without him having to actually ask the question. ''David said you are a terrific father to your two little boys, so I knew you'd be up on the schools. So, what school do they attend?''

He shrugged. ''They aren't in school yet.''

''But I thought David said they were around five?''

''They're four. They'll be five in a few months.''

''But at that age…'' She shrugged, obviously bothered. ''Surely they're on the list?''

''They're on the list for kindergarten in the fall,'' he said. ''And they're pretty excited about it, at least

Greg is. Gabe isn't so sure he wants to go, but if his brother goes, he'll tag along.''

"Oh, what school?" she asked, her interest piqued again.

"The elementary school near where we live."

"Public school?" she gasped, as if he'd said they were going into a labor camp. "Why would you do that?"

He drank more of the wine that the waiter had just poured for him. "It's the school my wife and I planned on for them."

Francine sat back, looking a bit flustered. "I'm sorry. That was insensitive of me. David explained about your loss, how your wife was…taken, and you were left with the two boys." She reached out and patted his hand again. An action he knew was an attempt to show sympathy, but it felt intrusive and wrong to him, the way her words did. "I'm sure things would be different if she was still…here."

If Gabriella was here, the boys would still be going to that school, and he wouldn't be enduring this stupid conversation with a woman who was looking for a sperm donor. He moved his hand away and sipped more wine before he said, "Yes, things would be very different."

"How long has it been since she…she passed?"

Passed? Was taken? "Since she died?" he asked bluntly, and wished he had more to drink.

"Yes," Francine murmured somberly.

"Almost two years," he said. Then his cell phone rang, and he took it out of the pocket of his dark suit coat as if he'd been thrown a lifeline. He glanced at the LED readout and saw a Houston number he recognized. That of Zane Holden, the CEO at LynTech Corporation, and a man who had proved to be a good friend to him when he needed one.

"Excuse me for a minute," he said to Francine. "I need to take this." He flipped the phone open and answered it. "Zane?"

"Yes, it's me, Rafael."

Zane was the only person who ever called Rafe by his given name, except for his mother. He'd said it fit, with Rafe's naturally bronzed skin, the ebony hair, black eyes and high cheekbones. Rafe didn't know if it fit or not, but it felt right coming from a friend he'd known since the very early days of his career in corporate security. They hadn't seen each other recently, not since Zane had gotten married, but they kept in touch.

"What's going on?" he asked, ignoring the waiter setting plates of food before them on the table.

There was no friendly small talk. "I need to speak with you as soon as possible. When can we get together?"

"What's going on? You and Lindsey—"

"No, it's business, and I need your help."

It was a given Rafe would do anything for Zane personally or on a business level. Zane had been the one to drag him back into the land of the living when he'd needed it the most. He glanced at Francine, who was picking at her meal and trying to appear not to be listening to his conversation. He wasn't about to feel guilty, only relieved that he had the perfect excuse to leave. "I'll call you back in five minutes."

"Five minutes," Zane said.

Rafe flipped the phone shut and smiled apologetically at Francine. At least he hoped he pulled that off. "I'm so sorry, but a business emergency just came up. I need to go."

"Oh, yes, okay," she said, and would have stood, but he motioned for her to remain where she was.

"No, you stay and enjoy your dinner." They'd come in their own cars, so that wasn't a problem. "Please, it's paid for."

She hesitated, then sank back in the chair, obviously not happy, but not about to make a scene. "Okay, but call me?"

He nodded, not about to agree to a lie out loud, then left. He settled the bill on the way out, and exited into the softness of the Fort Worth night. He gave the valet his parking ticket, then stood off to one side of the entry door. The night was balmy and clear, with a huge moon hanging over the city. He was obscenely relieved to be done with his first and last blind date, and actually felt as if he could breathe again. Then he flipped open his phone and hit Zane's number on speed dial. The CEO answered on the first ring.

"It's me," Rafe stated.

"Thanks for calling back," Zane said, while Rafe watched a black Jaguar pull up to the restaurant.

"No problem. Now what's wrong?"

Two women got out of the sleek black car, handed their keys to the valet, then walked toward the entry. One was tall and leggy, the other shorter and more compact. Both were blond and dressed to kill.

"A security leak at LynTech," Zane was saying in his ear.

"Let me give you Hal Simmons's private number and he can take care of things."

"No, I need you on it," Zane said.

Rafe had been watching the blondes, and was taken aback when the tall one stopped about three feet from him and very deliberately gave him the once-over. Her eyes roamed every inch of his six-foot-two-inch frame, skimming over his dark suit, the white, collarless silk shirt, then met his gaze. She didn't even blink.

"I don't get involved," he said into the phone to Zane, but realized he meant it with the woman, too. And she was waiting for him to say something to her directly, anything so she could come closer. But she'd have to wait until it snowed in July for that to happen. Not because she wasn't beautiful, but because he really wasn't interested in dating.

"I know you gave up working on the front line years ago, but I need you to come on down here and take a personal look at the situation," Rafe was saying through the phone. "I need your input. Nothing against your people, but you're the best, and I need you to do this."

"My people are good," he said, and realized his SUV was being brought up to the curb right then.

"Of course they are. That's why you're our security company at LynTech." Rafe listened as he straightened, then moved toward the blonde. She actually started to smile, but that didn't last when he walked right past her to get to his car. He thought he heard her mutter, "Whatever," but he didn't bother to check.

"Then let my crew deal with it," he said into the phone.

"No, no," Zane exclaimed as Rafe slipped into his black SUV and handed the valet a tip before the man closed his door for him. "I'd come up there to go over it with you, but Lindsey's pretty sick with this pregnancy."

Maybe if Zane hadn't mentioned Lindsey's sickness, Rafe would have tried to talk him into contacting Simmons. His friend's words stopped him. Rafe drove away from the restaurant into light traffic, remembering how sick Gabriella had been during her whole pregnancy with the twins, and how important it had been for him to be there for her. Despite being the head of Dagget Security, Inc., he'd stepped away from the hands-on operations of the company and started delegating and supervising so he could be with Gabriella. He'd never gone back to the day-to-day work and had never regretted his decision.

"It's that bad?" he asked as he headed west for home.

"Looks that way. We ducked the last disaster, but there's more coming. I can feel it. I'd hoped you could cover it yourself, maybe work out of this office for a few weeks."

Rafe hesitated, knowing that at any other time he would have rejected that idea out of hand. But he didn't this time. The fact was, he didn't need to get out and date and meet women to get on with his life. He needed to get out, period. Out of Fort Worth and out of the office. He'd go to Houston, and he'd take a break. The boys weren't in school yet, and it wouldn't be too hard to take them with him once he opened the house he had down there. They could even have their horses if they wanted to.

"I'll have to make arrangements for the boys and—"

"If you bring them along, why not use our day care center at the head office? It's top-notch and right in the building. Walker loves it there, and you'd be close if the boys needed you."

Rafe had met Walker, Zane's two-year-old son, shortly after Zane and Lindsey had married. Now Zane was going to be a father again. Strange how people you never thought of as parent material took to having kids like ducks to water.

The traffic slowed a lot and Rafe eased along the street at a snail's crawl, then made his decision. "Okay, I'll give it a shot. I'm not sure when I can get there."

"Just let me know. I'll set up a board meeting and—"

"No, don't do that." If he was going to handle this, he knew exactly how he'd work it. "I think I want to go in quietly and get the lay of the land. My men are already on your payroll for security, so I'll go in as one of them. No one would know the difference, and no one at LynTech would know me, except you and Lindsey. I can slip in easily."

Zane didn't argue. "Okay, when?"

"I'll get myself hired as soon as I hang up now. I can be in Houston in a couple of days, start working at LynTech and get everything set for Carmella to bring the boys down later.''

He heard Zane exhale with undisguised relief. ''Do you need me to do anything on this end?''

''Not yet. I'll let you know.''

''Okay, but I'll be in and out. Use my cell number. There's a huge charity ball LynTech is sponsoring to help the children's wing at the hospital and to fund the day care center. Lindsey's in the middle of it, and she's been so sick that I'm doing some of the footwork for her, anything to ease the burden on her. It's going to be huge.''

That gave Rafe another idea. ''When's the ball?''

''Next Saturday. It's at the E. J. Sommers's estate outside the city.''

''Who's doing security?''

''As a matter of fact, Dagget Security is donating their services. You're getting a huge tax write-off.''

Rafe hadn't been told about this charity donation, but he was glad someone in his company had thought of it. This would work perfectly. ''Are your people going to be at it?''

''It's practically a command performance for all departments and their heads, along with the rich and generous in the city.''

Rafe didn't know too many people in Houston, and if he was in a guard uniform, even the people who might know him wouldn't look at him twice. He outlined his idea to go in as one of the security staff and work the ball to get the lay of the land and to see the people firsthand. ''But I'll need personnel files on the top people in each department, along with their clearances, especially in Legal, Contracts, and anyone you think has access to the material that's being leaked. Throw in any computer gurus, and try to get pictures with each file.''

"It's done. You'll have it when you get here."

"I'll fly in Monday."

"That's great," Zane said. "How long do you think you can hang out around here?"

Rafe took a breath and slowed as he neared the fork in the road that headed south to Houston or west to his ranch. He swung toward the ranch. "As long as it takes," he murmured, not sure if he meant as long as it took to figure out what was going on with LynTech or as long as it took him to want to come back to Fort Worth.

Chapter One

Houston, a week later

Megan Gallagher adjusted the earpiece for her cell phone as she drove away from Houston in her rental car. She clicked a button on the microphone and said two words: "Ryan. Home."

"Calling Ryan home," a computerized voice said in her ear.

There were two rings, then Ryan Prescott Baron answered the phone in his usual way. "Baron here."

"Well, hello, Baron. Gallagher here," she said as she drove up the on-ramp and into freeway traffic heading west.

"You landed okay?"

"Sure. Some security breach held up takeoff for three hours, but I got some work done at the airport, and I finally arrived here." She settled back in the seat, barely taking in her surroundings as she drove.

"Are you at the hotel?"

"No, I'm on my way to a charity ball."

"A what?"

"When I got in, I received a message from Wayne Lawrence, the head of Legal for LynTech. A command to appear at this ball, wearing something fancy. It's black-tie, so I had to get a dress at the boutique at the hotel." A shimmering silver cocktail dress falling to just above her knees, with a low neck, deep back and narrow straps. The bill would go into her business expense folder when she got back to San Francisco. "The ball's a big event, and apparently everyone who's anyone at LynTech is going to be there. From the sound of it, I don't think anyone was given a choice. Mr. Lawrence didn't give *me* a choice, that's for sure."

"Did he fix you up with an escort, too?"

Ryan and she had known each other for three years, almost from the time she'd been recruited by LynTech out of law school into their San Francisco branch offices. She and Ryan had been engaged for the past month. They understood each other, and he understood what she had to do. He knew the rules of business. He played by them every day as the vice president of a large import-export company in the city. He knew that if this was a command performance by a superior, chances were she'd be paired up with someone else who was in the same boat. Thank goodness that hadn't happened.

"No, he didn't fix me up," she said, and scanned the signs coming into view.

The last time she'd been "fixed up" had been in law school, when her roommate had decided that she needed a social life and matched her with a recent graduate. Morris, she thought his name had been. No, Norris. And Norris had been divorced with three kids, and after the first excruciatingly boring hour, she'd finally realized that he was frantically looking for a woman to take the pressure off of him with his kids so he could further his career. She hadn't let herself be talked into a blind date again and never would. "I figure I'll get there, meet whomever I need to, memorize some names, then plead jet lag and leave."

"Now, that sounds like a plan," Ryan murmured. "Too bad I couldn't get away, or I could be your excuse to leave."

They played well off of each other at business functions. Another way they were well-matched. "I'll do this on my own," she said. "Don't worry about it." She'd been "doing" it on her own most of her life. Her parents had been middle-aged by the time Megan made her appearance. And her only brother headed out for college before she even got home from the hospital. She was very used to being on her own. "The jet lag excuse is just fine."

"Sorry, I've got another call coming in. Probably Brandson. I've been waiting for his update," Ryan said suddenly.

"Okay, go take your call."

"And you go to your ball," he said.

"Love you," she stated quickly.

"Same here," he answered. Then the line went dead.

She pushed the phone's Off button, then gripped the steering wheel again, the diamond on her ring finger glittering in the low light. She held her hand up in front of her. Ryan's grandmother's engagement ring, the Baron diamond, was on her finger now. Four carats, marquise cut. And sometime, somewhere down the road, his grandmother's wedding band with inset diamonds in platinum would join it.

It had been a good decision to accept his proposal. In a few years, they'd get married, and that would be a good decision, too.

They hadn't told too many people about the engagement, not even her brother or her parents. Megan told herself she wanted to give them the news in person, but she knew she was hesitant to tell them at all because they'd ask all the wrong questions. Quint especially. He'd had a bad marriage early on, and hadn't been terribly romantic. But when he'd met his new wife, the man had turned into a moonstruck Romeo. All he did was talk about Amy and the two kids they had.

And their mother would go on and on about "being in love" and how exciting and wonderful it was. Being in love was nice, Megan thought. Nice and sensible. That's what she and Ryan had. Nice and sensible, and if people found that boring, so be it. It worked for them.

She glanced at the clock on the dash of the rental car and grimaced. Mr. Lawrence had requested her presence at the ball by "no later than nine." It was already eight-thirty, and she still hadn't found the right exit to get to the E. J. Sommers's estate. She'd been born and raised in the Houston area before leaving six years ago, but she hadn't recognized the name of the road to the estate from the directions she'd been given.

"Meet me on the lower terrace," had been included in the note, too. She didn't know where the lower terrace would be. She'd never met Wayne Lawrence. But she'd find both the man and the lower terrace as soon as she found the estate.

She shifted, adjusted the hem of her dress, then glanced at herself in the rearview mirror. She'd chosen simple over fussy, confining her shoulder-length blond hair in a French twist held by diamond clips. She'd brushed color on her lips, put on a hint of mascara, and her only jewelry was the ring.

She looked ahead and saw a sign. The right road. She took the off-ramp onto a narrow, two-lane highway and turned the only way she could, south. As she drove around a curve, she sighed with relief when she saw the glow of lights ahead on the right, at the same moment she noticed a sign by the side of the road: Charity Ball, with an arrow pointing straight ahead.

She followed it, and pulled into an expansive entry space paved with cobble stones and faced by massive wrought-iron gates framed by stone pillars. She stopped by another sign: Check In Here. But she didn't see anything except a security keypad. She hadn't been given a code of any type. She looked through the gates and saw the glow from the main house. Even from this distance she could see a lot of activity going on.

She reached for her purse to get out the embossed invitation Mr. Lawrence had sent over for her, figuring there might have been a code on it she'd missed when she'd read it earlier. She skimmed the card, but didn't see anything that resembled a code. All it said was: "Valet service at the ballroom entrance."

She pushed it back in the envelope, rolled down her window and heard the faint sounds of music and voices drifting on the evening air. She looked at the security pad and spotted a phone by the keys. She was reaching for it when a deep male voice startled her.

"Good evening." She turned to see a security guard on the other side of the gates, a tall man in the shadows, moving toward the left pillar. "I'll be right there," he said, then disappeared, only to reappear out of a gate set into the fence on the other side of the pillar.

He came toward her, backlit by the lanterns that framed the entry. "Am I glad to see you," she said as he got within a few feet of the car. She could see now that he was carrying a clipboard in one hand, and there were a gun and two-way radio at his waist.

"Sorry for the wait."

She had to crook her neck a bit to look up at him. He was probably over six feet, lean, in a tailored uniform, but between the night shadows and his uniform cap, his face was almost indistinguishable. "I just need to get in to the ball."

He came close enough to touch the frame of her window with one hand, and leaned nearer. "Okay, no problem," he said as she noticed how strong his hand looked, tanned, with square, short nails and a simple gold wedding band on the ring finger. "What's the name?"

"Megan Gallagher."

He pulled back and scanned the clipboard. "Sorry, ma'am, but you're not on my list."

"Look again. It's Gallagher," she said, then spelled it out for him very slowly.

"There are two Gallaghers on here and you're not one of them. In fact, they've already left."

She knew the two Gallaghers—her brother, Quint, who'd been doing work for LynTech for a while, and Amy. Megan had thought they were in New York, but they must have come back for the ball. "Look again," she said, feeling a bit irritated that someone had forgotten to put her name on the list, and that she was now at the mercy of this guard. It was almost nine and she was going to be late.

She wasn't aware she'd said anything else out loud, but he stated, "If you're not on the list, you're not," as he hunkered down by the door. "Sorry."

The dim glow from the inside lights of the car touched his face, and she saw she was being assessed by dark, dark eyes under a slash of equally dark eyebrows. His clean-shaven face looked almost ethnic, with high cheekbones, deeply tanned skin and a strong jaw. And it fell just short of being handsome. No, it was more disturbing than handsome, and she didn't know why. "I need to get inside," she said with more bluntness than she'd intended.

"Not without your name being on this list."

"Oh, just let me in," she said.

"Sorry, I have strict orders not to let anyone in without being on the list."

He was like a broken record. Then she had an idea. She grabbed the invitation off the seat by her purse and turned to where he still crouched by her door. She thrust the printed card at him. "Here, this proves I'm supposed to be in there."

He took it from her and read it, while she frantically looked at the clock again and realized she was now officially late for her meeting. Then he held it back out to her. "Your name's not on this," he said. "You could have picked it up out of the trash."

That was it; she'd had enough. She opened the door, not caring if she hit him in the process, and climbed out. Her first realization when she faced him was that he was big. The security guard was over six feet tall, with broad shoulders well defined by the tight, tailored uniform. And he was annoyed. It was obvious by his stance and by the way his right hand clenched at his side. He let the invitation fall to the ground between them, then he crossed his arms on his chest, a power pose if ever she saw one. At least he didn't pull his gun.

"What's your name?" she asked, lifting her chin slightly and fighting the urge to cross her arms the way he had.

"Rafe Diaz," he said, then slowly spelled it out, letter by letter, as she had done with her name earlier. Then he asked, "Is this a standoff?"

"No, it's a problem," she said.

"I agree," he murmured without any sign of hesitation. "It's your problem."

"No, it's yours. You're being paid to let in guests, to be polite and make life simpler for the people going through these gates tonight, and because of you, I'm late for my date."

''Late for your date,'' he echoed, then quite deliberately let his gaze slide over her.

Her stomach clenched at the action, but she stood very still until he was finished and looked her in the eye again. ''Yes, late, and it's your fault.''

''I don't think laying blame is the best idea, so why don't we get past that and you tell me what you think I should do to be polite and make life simpler for you…without losing my job in the process?''

He was so composed that it only made her more annoyed. She frowned at him. ''Call someone,'' she said. ''That won't jeopardize your job, will it?''

''I don't know until you tell me who to call.''

Damn him. She crossed her arms on her breasts and kept her gaze level with his. ''Your boss.''

He shook his head. ''Not on a Saturday night. Not a good idea. That would jeopardize my job. Give me another person to call.''

She was tall, probably five feet ten inches without the flimsy silver heels she was wearing, and she kept her gaze locked with his as she nibbled on her full bottom lip. Damn, she was gorgeous in that shimmery dress, which did nothing to minimize her high breasts and the flare of her hips. Or legs that looked as if they could go on forever. Drop-dead gorgeous, and a royal pain. Whoever had given her the huge diamond flashing on her finger would have his hands full.

''Wayne Lawrence,'' she said suddenly. ''Call him. He's the one I'm meeting inside.'' She cocked her head to one side, and even in the dim light, he could see the way she arched one finely defined eyebrow. ''And don't tell me *he's* not on your list.''

Rafe had never liked women like this, women who felt as if they were entitled to have everyone bow and scrape before them. And he'd had enough of being ordered around by her. He'd make the call and get her out of here, one way or the other. "Okay," he said, and moved to the call box on the security pad. As he picked up the house phone, he thought he heard her sigh. A soft sound, not one of anger or exasperation, but one that meant she was tired or worried. It touched something in him, and he didn't want that at all.

He didn't turn, but grasped the phone and pushed in the number they'd given him for contact with security in the house. He identified himself and said, "Find Wayne Lawrence and ask him to confirm a Megan Gallagher as his guest."

"Where is he?" the voice on the other end asked.

"How would I know where he is?" Rafe practically snapped.

He felt a touch on his arm at the same time he heard Megan say, "He's waiting on the lower terrace by the ballroom."

He looked down at her, at her hand on his sleeve— the hand with the huge diamond on it—then at her. She drew back, breaking the contact quickly. "That's where he is?"

He saw her put her hand behind her back. "That's where he said we should meet," she murmured.

He gave the information to the man on the other end, then waited while he found Wayne Lawrence. Rafe was more than aware that Megan was still close to him, her delicate flowery scent touching the evening air. He knew it was her scent without even checking, but it didn't match her. The aroma was soft and very feminine, and she was definitely not soft. Feminine? Hell, yes, she was that in spades.

"Yeah, she's confirmed as his guest," the other guard said as he came back on the line. "He wants her let in and escorted to the lower terrace right away. So bring her on up."

"But I'm on the gate."

"Brad's coming down. He'll be there any minute. You come on back here with Miss Gallagher as soon as Brad gets there." Brad, another guard, had accepted Rafe as a co-worker with no idea who he really was. Only Zane knew Rafe's true identity and that he was using a fake last name.

Rafe put the phone back in its nook, then turned to Megan and finally put two and two together. Wayne Lawrence and Megan Gallagher? He didn't like the way that added up at all. He'd seen the photos of Mr. Lawrence. The man was sixty, maybe five-eight or so, almost bald, with a rumpled look about him. But he was high up in LynTech, a mover and a shaker. And you never knew about women. Maybe the power or the money or both were an aphrodisiac. But the idea of Megan Gallagher with this man brought a bitter taste to Rafe's mouth.

He turned to Megan, who had backed up a few paces while he'd been talking, a slender figure in the darkness. He tried not to notice any more about her, especially not the way the ring sparkled on the hand that held the forgotten invitation, which she'd picked up. "Well?" she asked.

"Wayne Lawrence is waiting," he murmured.

"So, you're going to open the gate for me?"

"Sure," he said. "And that's not all."

She hesitated before asking, "What does that mean?"

"You've got an armed escort."

"I what?" He could see her eyes widen. He wondered what color they were, and if it was just the night that made her lashes look so long and lush.

"He requested that you be escorted up to the house and taken to him on the lower terrace."

"No thanks, I can find it," she said quickly. Too quickly.

"I wouldn't bet on that. That house up there is the size of a small country."

"I'll take my chances," she said, then got back in her car. "Now, if you could just open the gates?"

She was making her escape, and he was inclined to let her go and find her way on her own. And he probably would have, but Brad McMillan, his replacement, came through the side gate right then. "Hey, Rafe, you can get going now."

"Okay," he said, then pushed the code for the main gates and went around in front of her car to get in on the passenger side. If she took off, she'd have to run him down to do it. Thankfully, she waited until he opened the door, and she even reached out and picked up her purse and cell phone to clear the seat for him. She dropped them on the center console along with the invitation before she put the car in gear.

"You all get going," Brad said through the open window. "Mr. Lawrence is really anxious for her to get up there."

"You didn't have to come with me," she said, as they eased through the open gates.

"I told you, I don't want to lose my job, and those were the orders—to deliver you up to Mr. Lawrence." She darted him an angry glance, and he said quickly, "Sorry, bad choice of words."

"Sure you're sorry," she muttered, and even though she was angry now, it didn't stop his body tensing when he noticed the way her dress was riding up her thigh. This had been a mistake. But he was in it now and he'd get out as soon as he could.

"I really am sorry," he said.

"You're just sorry that I really do have a right to be going to the ball."

"Well, you're no Cinderella," he said.

She cast him a quick look. "I'm not wearing glass slippers, true," she said before she turned back to the driveway ahead of them.

"Can I make a suggestion?" he asked.

"Could I stop you?"

"No, you couldn't. I was just going to say that the jewelry doesn't work with that dress."

Very casually, she took her left hand off the wheel and rested it on her thigh, effectively hiding the ring from him. "What about my jewelry?"

"That earpiece just doesn't do anything for you."

She reached for the device connected to her cell phone and tugged it free, then dropped it on the console with her other things. "I forgot," she said. "I got distracted."

He found himself smiling. He was distracted, too, by a woman who was thoroughly stuck-up and bossy.

The thing was, he was enjoying it. He hadn't sparred verbally with a woman for a very long time, and he realized that he'd missed it. Even if she was annoying and what his mother used to call ''uppity.'' And even if he'd never see her again. Not that he wanted to. But this was a nice distraction for a few minutes.

They were almost up the driveway now, and he pointed ahead to the portico just outside the ballroom entrance. ''Pull in there and the valet can park your chariot for you.''

Rafe was shocked when she actually laughed, a soft, sultry sound that seemed to fill the space around him as she pulled up to the nearest valet. That was when he looked at her, and he saw her smiling at him. A simple smile, yet it triggered so many things deep inside him that he found it hard to breathe. ''Let me guess. Chariot parking is not part of your job description?''

And responding to this woman on such a basic level wasn't something he wanted to do. ''No,'' he said, and the second the car stopped, he got out.

The air was filled with laughter and music and the scent of good cigars, but all he was aware of was Megan coming around the car when the valet let her out, and Megan standing in front of him with her purse clutched to her middle, the shadow of that smile still on her lips. And the gleaming ring on her finger. He looked away out of self-preservation, saw her car being driven off for parking, then said, ''Follow me,'' without looking at her again. ''I'll take you to Wayne Lawrence. That *is* in my job description,'' he said, and started off without looking to see if she was following.

Actually, he didn't have to look to know she was there. He could sense her, and he kept going, through the service area, around the side of the mansion, toward the back terraces. They walked along a pathway that cut across grass and through low shrubbery, and as they turned at the back corner of the house, she brushed against him. Rafe moved quickly ahead of her onto the flagstone terrace.

The party had spilled out onto the back lawns, under the draped fairy lights, and with the French doors of the ballroom, the music seemed to be everywhere, mingled with laughter. He stopped at the edge of the terrace, scanning the groups of guests to try and spot Wayne Lawrence. Sensing Megan right beside him, Rafe turned and saw her features softly illuminated in the glow of the lights. Blue. Her eyes were a clear blue, and that damn ring was winking at him. "I can take it from here," she said. "Thanks for the escort."

"Sorry for the trouble at the gate."

"You were doing your job," was all she said, as loud laughter from the far side of the terrace drew her attention. A group of people stood there—all men, all drinking, he noted—and that was when he spotted Mr. Lawrence. Rafe had only seen him in the picture Zane had provided, but recognized the man immediately. He looked every day of his sixty years, balding as he was, and even though the picture had been head and shoulders, Rafe had guessed right about him being out of shape despite the very expensive tux he was wearing.

"Well, there he is," he said to Megan, motioning to Mr. Lawrence. "You found him on the lower terrace."

"Yes, I did," she murmured.

Right then, another security guard came jogging from the upper terrace, skirting the guests by staying on the lawn. Seeing Rafe, he hurried over and said in a low voice, "A 215 at the Service."

That was their code for a troublesome drunk—a way of communicating what was going on without the guests knowing. Rafe had started that practice when he'd actually worked the events, the way he was doing tonight. "The Service" meant the problem was at the delivery area.

He nodded to the guard. "I'll be right there," he said, and the other man took off while he turned back to say goodbye to Megan.

But she was gone. He looked across the terrace and saw her approaching Mr. Lawrence with her hand out. A big smile was on his face.

There was no backward glance, no hesitation on her part. Rafe was forgotten, a security guard who had bugged her, then escorted her to her date. And that was okay. He didn't plan on remembering too much of what happened tonight, either. He headed toward the front of the house in a jog to help take care of the drunk.

Chapter Two

Monday

Megan was in her office, one of the dozen or so cubicles just off the main hallway, and right next to the rest rooms for the entire floor. Little more than three partial walls with no door, it was stocked with the usual office equipment, along with a stack of work that had been sent to her that morning. The only good thing about her work area was the window, even if it did look out onto the roof of the building next door.

Not that she had much time to look out the window. She'd been busy since she'd arrived, and was still facing two or three hours of work she'd have to take back to the hotel with her when she left.

"That was certainly a lovely party."

Megan looked up to find her boss in the doorless entry. The receptionist, Ellen, who sat at a desk directly across from the elevators, had told Megan earlier that Mr. Lawrence liked to keep an eye on "his people." She'd made a joke about him wearing a bell

around his neck so staff would be warned when he
was closing in. Megan had thought she'd been kidding, but now she knew the woman had been serious.
Megan hadn't heard the man approach.

"Oh, sir," she said, pushing back the file she was
reading, the details of the day care center incorporation
to separate it from LynTech. "I didn't hear you come
in." She brushed at her hair, which she'd caught in a
low knot that morning, and tugged a bit nervously at
the cuffs of the simple white shirt she was wearing
with beige linen slacks.

"I'm sorry," he said as he came into the cubicle.
But he didn't sound any sorrier for his actions than
Rafe had Saturday night. Now why had she thought
of the security guard? "I just wanted to make sure
everything was going well for you, and to say it was
a pleasure meeting you at the ball."

"Oh, thank you so much." She'd left the event as
soon as she could, but not before Mr. Lawrence had
pulled her from group to group, introducing her to so
many people she couldn't remember any of them. All
she really remembered was a glimpse of Rafael Diaz
going past the French doors just as Mr. Lawrence had
taken her hand to tug her over to yet another group of
guests. She'd seen a flash of a frown on the guard's
face, then he'd disappeared for the rest of the evening.
"The ball was wonderful."

Mr. Lawrence, dapper in a solid navy suit, matching
tie and gray shirt, came to the front of her desk. "I
was very glad you finally showed up." He hadn't been
annoyed by her tardiness, but seemed to appreciate the

guard being so careful with her entry to the ball. "Better safe than sorry," he murmured soberly.

"Absolutely," she said, not sure if she should stand or not.

He took that decision out of her hands when he motioned for her to stay sitting, then said, "I just came in to say that we're glad you're here, and this month should prove illuminating for everyone." He tapped at his wristwatch with his forefinger. "It's seven, and you're the last one still here. I appreciate dedication, and it will go in your file."

Was that why he'd come by? Because he'd noticed her light on when the other cubicles were dark? She pressed a hand to the papers in front of her. "I wanted to finish up the first part of the file you gave me before I left."

"I was hoping I'd catch you and save you a trip to the hotel to get your things."

She didn't understand. "Is there a problem?"

"Oh, no. I just wanted to let you know that your belongings from the hotel were moved to the loft this afternoon, to save you the trouble. They should be there when you arrive."

He'd called her to his office earlier and informed her that she was moving out of the hotel to a loft the company used. He'd explained it was wired directly to the offices, and to the legal department in particular. The rationale for the move was so she could access the database of both the day care center and LynTech anytime she wanted to from there, and the inference was she could work even if she wasn't at the office. The details of the switch to independent status for the day care center was tedious but necessary work, and the reason she'd been sent to Houston.

She hadn't thought much about it until that moment, but suddenly felt uneasy that a perfect stranger had gone into her hotel room and packed her things for her. But she forced herself to smile. "Thanks for taking care of that for me," she said, and hoped she didn't choke on the words.

"You're very welcome," he answered. Then he looked at his watch again. "Oh, my. I need to run. I'm meeting Abe Larson in half an hour." She had no idea who Abe Larson was, but didn't have a chance to ask before he said, "I'll see you back here first thing in the morning."

"Yes, sir," she murmured, but found herself speaking to his retreating form as he left.

She sank back in her chair, then swiveled it toward the window and looked out at the starry sky and partial moon that hung over the city below. She'd almost forgotten how beautiful Houston looked. She'd been gone for so long and had only came back when her mother insisted she visit. San Francisco was her home now, and Megan had hopes that if she proved herself this month, she'd be promoted in the San Francisco offices.

As she twisted the diamond on her finger absent-mindedly, she felt a sudden need to talk to Ryan. She wanted to hear his voice. But when she turned to reach for her briefcase and her cell phone, she had a flashing memory of Rafe looking at her ring. Of his joke about her earpiece, and his teasing about a chariot and Cinderella.

She took a deep breath and banished that night from

her thoughts. Taking out her phone and turning it on, she dropped it in the pocket of her shirt and hooked the earpiece in place. But before she could press the microphone button and give the command to call Ryan, the device rang. She pressed the Receive button on the cord and said, "Hello?" not realizing how much she wanted it to be Ryan until she heard another voice.

"Meggie?"

Quint was the only one to call her Meggie, and he seldom phoned her. He was so busy with his new life, she seldom got a chance to talk to him. "I haven't heard from you since…oh, I remember," she said. "When you told me you were going to change diapers again, and that the adoption was going through."

"I did, and I am." He laughed, a rich sound on the line. "I finally remembered why you stand back when you diaper a boy."

It was her turn to laugh. "It'll come back to you, sort of like riding a bike. Trust your instincts," she said.

"Oh, I am," he said. "Now, where have you been? I've tried calling your place for hours, and your cell phone kept going to your voice mail."

"I was working and turned it off for a while," she said. "What's going on?"

"We just got into New York to get my things from the apartment, but I wanted you to be the first to know that—"

"Oh, no," she said, cutting him off as she sat upright in her chair. "You and Amy aren't pregnant, are you?"

There was total silence on the other end, then Quint said, "Not that I know of."

"Then what is it?"

"Amy and I are going to live at the ranch."

Megan wasn't surprised by their decision to take over the ranch where she'd been brought up. "I thought you might."

"I didn't think you had any interest in taking it over."

"I never even thought about it," she said truthfully. "And I don't think Ryan would go for the ranch life, anyway."

"What would he have to do with it?" Quint asked abruptly.

She hadn't meant to do this, but since the door was open, she plunged ahead. "We're engaged."

"Oh, Meggie," he murmured, then she heard him taking a rough breath. "Are you sure about this?"

"Absolutely."

"You love him?"

She knew he'd ask that. "Of course."

"Then I won't argue. So, when's the big day?"

"We haven't even started to figure out when. We're both trying to stabilize our careers."

"Now, that's romantic," Quint murmured.

She looked at the ring on her finger. "It's perfect."

"How about the folks?"

"I was going to tell them later on. I've got so much to do right now."

"The San Francisco offices are busy?"

"Actually, I'm in Houston for a month of training and evaluation."

That shocked him into silence for a moment. "Why didn't you let us know you were coming in? We could have stuck around for a few days," he finally declared. "But then, we'll be back in a few weeks."

"Great, but for now this is all work," she said. "Maybe next time."

"What's the evaluation for?"

"An opening up the ladder in contracts, incorporation and diversification. So I'm working on incorporation for part of LynTech. I think they want to make sure I can handle it, and I'm—"

"Hold it." He cut her off. "I get the idea. You're moving on up, aren't you?"

"Hopefully."

"And Ryan thinks this is...?" He let his voice trail off.

"Great. Wonderful. Fantastic."

"Good for him," her brother murmured, but didn't sound as if he meant it. Then he shifted gears. "So, where are you staying?"

"At some private loft the company has wired to the office."

"I've heard of it, but I'm not sure where it is."

"I can tell you in just a minute." She looked for the envelope Mr. Lawrence had given her earlier with the address, directions and two keys. She searched in her briefcase, then on the desk, but didn't see the envelope anywhere. She pulled open the desk drawer. Nothing. "I can't find the address or directions. But I'm heading there tonight. They already moved my things over. Listen, I need to get going."

"You're still at work?"

"I'm just leaving."

"Damn, you're as much of a workaholic as I used to be," he said. "But if you're serious about wanting this advancement, Zane Holden and I—"

"No, no, no," she said quickly. "I don't want you to talk to anyone about anything. I can do this, Quint."

"Of course you can," he said. "Old habits die hard. Being a big brother and all."

"I know. But please, just don't say anything to anyone about me being here, or mention that I'm your sister or anything. Okay?"

"Okay," he said. "But—"

She cut him off. "Give Amy and the kids my love. And let me know when you're moving onto the ranch."

"You got it," he said, and Megan ended the call.

She looked through her things one more time, then remembered where the envelope was. She'd left it in Mr. Lawrence's office, on the desk. She'd put it down when she'd picked up more files he'd given her, and she didn't remember picking it up again. Directions, keys and phone numbers were in it. "Damn it," she muttered, glancing out the entry to her cubicle. Mr. Lawrence was gone, but she hoped to heck that he didn't lock his office at night.

Seven o'clock. She just hoped her boss hadn't yet gone to meet Abe Larson. She left everything on her desk and hurried through the quiet legal department, out to the main hallway, then down to his office. She tried the outer door, and it opened. Then she crossed the reception area, tried his private office door and exhaled in a rush when she found it unlocked, too.

She looked inside and saw the room was empty. Hesitating, she finally stepped into the darkly formal area done in cherry wood, brass and various shades of beige and gold. Turning on the light, she crossed to the massive desk, disappointed to find no envelope there, just papers, folders and books neatly stacked on the polished surface. She went behind it, then tried the top drawers, but they were all locked. She reached for a deep drawer on the side, pulled on the handle and silently slid it open.

She saw a correspondence file, a stack of company calendars, what looked like an unused day planner, and boxes of paper clips—lots and lots of boxes of paper clips. But no envelope belonging to her. She reached for the drawer on the other side and opened it. Books and papers and more paper clips. And sitting in one corner, a small bottle of very expensive scotch with a single shot glass beside it. Mr. Lawrence had his vices, she thought in surprise. Two low drawers were closed and locked.

She looked at the desktop again, then went around to the In and Out baskets at the front of the desk. She rifled through the latter. Nothing there for her. "Great, just great," she muttered, reaching for the In basket.

She barely got her hand on the top papers when someone grabbed her from behind, a strong hand on her upper arm, and she instinctively jerked to free herself. But the action only intensified the other person's grip as he turned her around. She spun like a top, landing against a solid wall of strength with an impact that expelled the air from her lungs. Megan heard someone scream—was that her?—then the world seemed to stop in its tracks.

The "wall" she'd hit was in uniform, with no hat this time, but the same midnight-dark eyes. And his hand was holding her with a firmness that was just this side of inflicting pain. Rafe Diaz. Even larger than she remembered, and very real. She pushed away, freeing herself, and stumbled slightly, feeling the desk hit her at the hips. She pressed one palm to her chest.

Her heart hammered against her hand, and her breathing came in gulps. She'd never been so shocked in her life, or so unnerved by another person. And he looked as if everything was just fine, that it was entirely normal for him to accost her.

"What do you think you're doing?" she managed to gasp in a hoarse voice.

Rafe had known it was her as soon as he spotted her. Even if he couldn't see her face, and viewed her only from the back. Megan Gallagher. In Wayne Lawrence's office going through his desk.

Rafe was supposed to be at the house in Houston, helping Carmella, the nanny, settle the boys for the night, but instead he'd been stuck doing rounds because one of the scheduled guards hadn't shown up for work. It had been so long since he'd worried about schedules and time cards, but now, acting like any other employee, he was on the receiving end of an extended shift. But maybe it had paid off for him.

He'd come up here to check things out, make sure everything was shut up tight, and had seen the open door with Wayne Lawrence's name on the brass plaque. He knew Mr. Lawrence had left in a limousine half an hour ago. He'd watched him get into the long black car, and for a moment Rafe had wondered if Megan was in there, waiting for the man. Then he'd pushed that thought aside and started his rounds.

Now he knew where she was. Here. Going through Mr. Lawrence's papers, in his private office. Muttering softly under her breath.

He'd watched for a moment, a million things going through his mind. Rafe had tried to focus on possibilities. She was working with Mr. Lawrence, so he could have asked her to come up here. But why hadn't she left with him? Why was she in here alone, going through his desk? Maybe Mr. Lawrence's money and position weren't the drawing cards for her. Maybe it was what his position opened up to her.

Any idea Rafe came up with was distasteful, and the fact that she was attractive didn't help things. When she started rifling through the baskets, he knew he had to make a move. He'd come up behind her, taking in the way her slacks defined the swell of her hips, her shirt clung softly to her back and shoulders.

She hadn't even heard him coming. The instant he touched her, felt her softness and fine bones, she gasped and spun around sharply, trying to break his hold on her. The next moment she was pressed against his chest and he was staring into eyes every bit as blue as he'd thought they were Saturday night. And that scent was everywhere, although he was careful not to inhale too deeply.

She was as tall as he remembered, but the flash and glitter were gone. The shimmery silver dress was replaced by tailored slacks and a simple white blouse made of something soft that clung to her high breasts. The earpiece for her phone was in place again, and her hair was combed back from her flushed face. He couldn't tell if she had on lipstick or if her lips were that shade of pink naturally. And those eyes... Blue, and glaring at him as if he had two heads.

"What do you think you're doing?" she yelped in a breathless voice.

He pulled his hands back, clenching them. He was almost sure they were shaking slightly, and he didn't know why. "What do you think *you're* doing?" he countered.

Those blue eyes narrowed even more and he could see her take a deep breath that strained the fine material across her breasts. "You're the one who attacked me."

He almost felt a laugh coming on at the way her chin lifted a bit. "And you're the one standing in someone's private office, rifling through papers."

"I'm not rifling through anything, and for your information, I'm supposed to be here."

"Oh, and you're not on the sign-in list, either." He would have noticed her name if she'd signed in earlier in the day.

She closed her eyes for a long moment, then looked at him again as if gathering herself. "Okay, you've got yet another list that I'm not on. Just tell me what list you're talking about this time."

"Everyone who comes into the building is supposed to sign in at the desk or in the garage. We know at any given time everyone who's in the building. According to my lists, you're not in the building. Therefore, you aren't supposed to be here.''

"Forget it," she muttered, and turned to reach for the papers again. "I don't have time for your little power trips right now."

He moved closer to grasp her once more and this time the softness under his fingertip unnerved him. She jerked away from the contact, and if she'd been angry before, she was furious now. But he didn't back down. "Leave that alone," he ordered quietly.

"Don't you touch me again," she retorted through clenched teeth.

He tried to ignore the way she rubbed at her arm where he'd made contact, but he couldn't ignore the blush of high color on her cheeks, or the fact that it only made her more beautiful. "I won't touch you if you stop trying to go through the desk."

She closed her eyes for a fleeting moment, then opened them and took a breath. He was sure there was a shadow of a smile at the corners of her full lips. It was no wonder an older man would fall into her trap, if she used that smile to get to him. Then she spoke evenly and with a softer tone. "No doubt you're earning your wages, Mr. Diaz, and I'm sure protecting LynTech is right at the top of your job description. But in this instance, as in your actions Saturday night, you're wrong. I'm just trying to find something that was left here for me."

If she'd just smiled, he probably would have backed off. He would have shown her out and let it go. But she used that tone, the one that sounded polite and reasonable, but had an underlying hint of superiority and condescension. "What was he leaving for you—money, jewelry, keys to an apartment?"

She looked confused, until his sarcastic remark suddenly registered. Her cheeks dotted with even more color, and she lifted her hand as if to strike him. "You creep!" she cried as he caught her by her wrist.

"Don't even think of doing that." She jerked against his constraint and he released her. "You're out of here. Let's go."

"I'm not going anywhere with you," she exclaimed, rubbing at her wrist. "How dare you suggest that I...that Mr. Lawrence and I..." She shook her head as she hugged her arms tightly around herself. "That's sick."

"I'm sick? You're the one seducing a man old enough to be your father to get...whatever."

"Whatever?" she echoed.

He expected another explosion and braced himself, but when it came, the emotion wasn't anger. Instead she started laughing. "You're serious? You think that I—that..." Suddenly she smiled, the way she'd smiled in the car on Saturday night, a real expression of humor that quite literally took his breath away. "Me? You think that I'm...?" She shook her head. "You're so wrong."

On Saturday night he'd thought it was fun to spar with her, to bait her and joust with words, but he knew right now that he was out of his element. Rafe didn't want any part of her smile, or the way she made him feel completely off balance.

"Oh, I'm wrong, am I?" he muttered. "Then why

don't you explain things so this poor, lowly hired hand can understand?''

She didn't respond to his sarcasm, but leaned back against the edge of the desk. ''Okay, I'll put this simply. I work here. I just arrived Saturday, and had to go right to the ball to meet Mr. Lawrence, who is my boss, and someone I had never even seen before. I didn't, and still don't, know about signing in or signing out. That was one thing I wasn't told to do, and I imagine my name isn't on your endless list of lists for the same reason it wasn't on the list for the ball. Someone forgot to put it there.''

He folded his arms on his chest, fighting an odd impulse to brush at a stray strand of hair that had escaped her severe knot. ''Everyone employed by LynTech is on the list.''

''Not if someone messes up, which, since we're all human, people tend to do from time to time.'' She looked him right in the eye, and let a full second lapse for emphasis before she added, ''You must understand that concept.''

Sarcastic and superior. And gorgeous. What a waste of gorgeous, he thought. ''I understand that you aren't on the list.''

He quite enjoyed her losing control when she threw up her hands and muttered, ''You and your damn lists.''

No one had mentioned that she worked here, and when he'd told Zane about the ball, about her showing up, all his friend had said was, ''Everyone could invite a guest if they bought a ticket.'' And when Rafe had gone through the files on the work history of every employee, with pictures attached, he hadn't come across anything on Megan Gallagher. He sure as hell would have remembered that photo. "Bottom line, Miss Gallagher, you don't belong here."

She stood straight again, leaning closer, and she brought that scent with her. "I don't know what you want me to say or do. I'm new, so I'm not on the list. I'm also temporary, and I'm in here because Mr. Lawrence, who most definitely is no more to me than my boss for a month, gave me an envelope, which I forgot to take with me. Now I need it, so here I am."

She wasn't backing down, and truth be told, Rafe was wearing out. It had been fun for a while, maybe disturbing for most of the conversation, and definitely diverting, but he wanted this situation settled. "Why don't we just do the obvious thing—what we did Saturday night—and call Mr. Lawrence?" He motioned to the earpiece in her ear and the cell phone in her pocket. "Use your fancy equipment and give the guy a call?"

She put her hand over her breast, and he realized she was covering the phone in her pocket. "No, I won't."

It was his turn to get exasperated. "And why not?"

"Because he's my boss, and disturbing one's boss over something like this won't look good on my résumé."

He checked his watch. "It's just past seven o'clock and it's not a Saturday night," he pointed out. Then he reached around her to pick up the phone on the desk. "I'll do it."

"No, you won't," she said, moving with him. The

next instant she was against his side, her arm tangled with his and her hand covering the one that gripped the receiver. "No," she said again, right by his ear.

Feelings exploded in him, feelings he thought were dead and gone, buried along with Gabriella. Rafe felt Megan's breasts against his side, her hand touching his, her breath fanning his skin. Her scent filled his nostrils. His reaction was so sudden and intense it shook him to the core. He drew back, disentangled himself, and faced her. He was shaken and trying desperately to recover.

He'd gone from baiting her to wanting her in the most basic way. She was a total stranger, a woman who was opinionated, superior, condescending, infuriating and incredibly desirable. A woman who made his whole body ache with need, and who warmed his soul. A woman who filled his mind with searing images of the two of them joining together....

He covered his left hand with his right, felt the smooth gold of his wedding band and swallowed, hard.

"Don't call Mr. Lawrence," she said, and it sounded as if she was speaking from a great distance, down a long tunnel.

She touched her tongue to her lips, and he could almost imagine the taste of her, as crazy and impossible as that was. She was clearly waiting for his next move, and he didn't know what that would be. He saw her exhale, and could swear he felt her breath brush his skin. He must be insane. His world had just exploded into something he didn't recognize.

The need in him was painfully raw and basic, but

it was wrong. It didn't matter that it seemed to have a life of its own, that it had burst into his reality, distracting him completely. Megan was a woman who didn't give a damn about him. And he needed to force himself to stay neutral. But as she stood straighter, reducing some of the space between them, he knew he couldn't. That was impossible. As impossible as wanting a woman like her.

Chapter Three

Megan stared at Rafe, not certain what was going on. But she wanted out of here. The room seemed closed and airless. She found that breathing wasn't easy for her, and she spoke quickly. "You don't want to bother Mr. Lawrence if you don't have to." She inhaled a deep breath. "I'm here for training and possibly evaluation for a promotion, and if you call him…" She shrugged, already saying more than she should have. "Please, just let me find the envelope and you can read what's in it before I take it. Okay?"

He didn't move. He just stared at her, his hands behind his back, then he spoke in a low voice. "Find the damn envelope."

"Thank you," she said, and didn't waste any time before turning back to the desk to look for it. She went through everything twice, but no envelope appeared. Finally she moved some books aside and withdrew a stack of papers beneath them. There it was. The envelope even had her name on the front of it.

She turned and held it up to Rafe. "Here it is."

He looked at it, then came close enough to take it

from her. She watched him open the flap, pull out a sheet of paper and examine it. "According to this, Ms. Gallagher is being moved to another location so your time at LynTech can be spent more productively."

"See, I told you so," she said, and realized that sounded like a childish retort. "It's all there."

He looked back at the letter. "It's got directions." He frowned as he read silently. "That's a lousy area," he murmured before he looked back at her with those dark eyes. "Why are they putting you up there?"

"He said it's wired to the LynTech database, and I can work more effectively from there than I could from the hotel."

"Whatever," Rafe said, refolding the paper and putting it back in the envelope. Then he shook out two keys. "Front door and loft," he said as he read the tags. He dropped them back in the envelope and handed it to her. "Once again, I was wrong. You're right. You can go."

She expected to feel victorious, but didn't, thanks to the darkness in his eyes. She didn't understand that look at all, and normally wouldn't have cared. But for some reason, it bothered her. "Thank you," she said, holding on tightly to the envelope. "I just need to get my things from my cubicle, then I'll leave." She heard herself add, "And can you show me where to sign the list?"

She thought he might at least smile a bit at that, but all he said was, "Get your things and I'll sign you out."

"Okay," she agreed, and headed for the door.

He followed, but never came abreast of her all the

way to her cubicle. When she went inside he stayed at the doorless entry and silently watched as she got her briefcase and put her paperwork in it. She closed it and looked up to find him eyeing her intently. "Can I ask you one thing?" she murmured.

"What's that?"

"Why on earth would you assume that Mr. Lawrence and I were...together?"

He motioned to her hand. "I know that's an engagement ring, and since you were hunting for Mr. Lawrence at the ball, well..." He shrugged. "It wouldn't be the first time an older man and a younger woman got together."

She knew her face was getting red. "That's not the case," she said, and snapped the locks on the briefcase. "Not at all."

"That's not an engagement ring?" he asked.

"Of course it is. And for your information, my fiancé is thirty-three, five years older than I am." Why in the heck had she told him that? "But that's none of your business."

"I didn't ask," he pointed out.

"Do you need to see my ID or anything now?"

Rafe hesitated, then put out his hand. "Sure."

She opened the briefcase again, pulled out a slim wallet and took out her California driver's license. He looked at it and read aloud, "Megan Stanford Gallagher." Then he glanced up at her. "Stanford?"

She'd always hated her middle name. "My grandmother's maiden name."

"Oh, I thought you were named after the university," he said. "You know, Stanford University."

"No," she said.

"Okay. Just checking." Then he read, "Twenty-eight, five feet ten inches, a hundred and—"

She went around and snatched the license out of his hand. "I think that's enough," she said, and returned it to her wallet. "I'm who I said I am, and I'm here for the reason I told you."

She snapped the briefcase shut and heard Rafe repeat, "You are who you say you are, and you're here for the reason you told me."

"Thank you." She looked up at him. "Now, tell me if you're just overzealous about your job, or did you seriously think I was stealing company secrets?"

"The latter," he murmured.

"You are kidding, aren't you?"

"No."

"And you thought I was getting involved with Mr. Lawrence to ferret out company secrets?"

"That sounded reasonable to me," he said.

She shook her head. The thought was just plain sickening to her. "I'm ready to leave," she said, then saw the boxes she had to take with her. She pointed to them. "They need to go with me. Since you're here, and you have to sign me out, you can carry them down for me."

"I'm a guard, not a valet," he said, and didn't move.

She blinked at his words. She hadn't meant to offend him, or ask him to be her slave. "I just thought it would help me get out of here faster," she said with all honesty.

"Of course it would. Just ask me, instead of assuming I'll be your lackey."

She had no idea where this was coming from, but it made her feel uneasy. "I'm sorry," she said. "I'll take them myself and make a couple of trips."

That clearly wasn't the right thing to say, either, though she didn't know why. "It's going to kill you to be polite, isn't it?" he murmured in a low voice.

"Forget it. It won't kill me to make two trips." She glanced at her watch. "I'll be done in ten minutes, if that's okay with you?"

"Now's even better," he said, and went straight to the boxes, picking them up. "Let's get this over with."

He sounded as if he were about to have a root canal operation, but she didn't argue. She collected her things, then did as he said, leading the way to the elevators. She reached to press the down button, and the doors opened immediately. She stood back to let Rafe on board, then followed and hit the button for the lobby.

She faced the doors as they closed, and deliberately didn't look at Rafe's reflection in them as he stood beside her. The elevator started down, and she realized she might not be looking at him, but he was staring at her. "What?" she finally said.

"Excuse me, ma'am?"

"Why are you staring at me like that?"

"Sorry," he murmured, and as she eyed him, he glanced away. "I was just thinking that if I were you, I wouldn't wear a ring like that in the neighborhood you're going to tonight."

"What does that mean?"

"How big is that ring?" he asked.

"None of your business," she said.

"Three carats, four?" he pressed.

"Big enough."

"Okay, a nice ring. The place you're staying is in a fringe area, a mixture of warehouses and converted lofts, populated with homeless street people."

She knew the type of area, but had assumed that the loft was in an industrial section that had been turned into pricey condos and studios. "Mr. Lawrence arranged it, and I don't think he would put me in a place he considered questionable or unsafe."

"It might be paradise," Rafe said, staring straight ahead at the doors, "but I'd still keep that ring under wraps."

She covered the diamond with her other hand.

"One more suggestion?" he said, and this time he met her gaze in the reflection.

"What now?" she asked with a tinge of exasperation.

"When you park there, assuming they don't have a secured parking area, go right to the door and have your key ready. Then go straight in."

She frowned at him, hating the uneasiness that was beginning to niggle at her. "What are you trying to do, scare me as payback for…not signing the lists?"

He shrugged. "Security's my job, and I'm just giving you a few suggestions. Take them or leave them."

The elevator stopped and the doors opened with a soft chime. He let her step out first, then went with her to the back exit, toward the parking garage. Megan opened the door, let him go out, then followed, hearing the door close with a metallic clang. She headed for her car, parked between a foreign compact and a large black SUV.

She hit the lock release, then Rafe put the boxes on the back seat, closed the door and turned to her. "I would have pegged you for a BMW," he said.

"I have a Porsche," she admitted. "I flew in, so it couldn't come with me. This is a rental from the company."

He opened her door for her, and as she slipped into the driver's seat, he crouched by her the way he had at the entry gate that night. "Anything else, ma'am?" he asked in an annoyingly deferential tone that she knew he didn't mean at all.

"Nothing, thanks," she said, putting her briefcase on the passenger seat.

"Well, if you think of anything, give me a call," he said, and motioned to her phone and the earpiece. "You're wired for it."

"Sure, you'll be the first one I call if I need something," she muttered.

She was braced for some snappy comeback meant to cut her to the quick, but he surprised her when he said simply, "Be careful."

What looked like genuine concern touched his dark eyes, and that surprised her, too. He was taking this whole thing seriously, about security and the neighborhood. "I plan to be."

"Good. You do that," he said. "Do you know where you're going?"

"Excuse me?"

"How to get there, to the loft?"

"Oh. No." She turned to her briefcase, opened it and took out the now infamous envelope to get the letter and read it more carefully. There wasn't any mention of parking in it, but there were directions she could easily follow. "It's all here."

"One more thing?"

"What?"

"If you do end up parking on the street, don't leave anything in your car where it can be seen through the windows. You'd be asking for trouble."

"Are you sure you don't live down there or something?" she asked. "You seem to know a whole lot about the criminal element."

He stared at her, hard. Then he stood and said, as if from a great distance above her, "Why don't you call my parole officer and ask him about me?" Slamming the door so hard it shook the car, he strode away without looking back.

Megan was stunned. She hadn't meant anything by what she'd said, but he was furious at her. Offended, obviously. And walking away. She scrambled out of the car and called to him as he got to the door of the building. "Hey, I didn't sign the damn list!"

He stopped, then turned. "You never checked in, so technically you aren't here. You don't exist." And he left.

She sank back into the car, horrified to feel her eyes smarting with tears. She swiped at them. She never cried. Never. But now she was on the verge of springing a leak. She could hate him, really hate him, for the way he got to her.

She put the car in gear and headed for the exit. Maybe she wouldn't see him again. It looked as if he worked nights, and she wasn't about to stay late anymore. She wouldn't have to with the setup at the loft.

She got to the closed security gate and it didn't move to open. She realized she didn't know what to do to get out. She'd come in with other cars that morning.

She spotted a keypad by an empty booth, rolled down the window and leaned out to examine it. One of the buttons was labeled Assistance, and she pressed it. She pressed it again, and still nothing happened. Everyone must be gone for the night and she was stuck.

She sank back in the seat and felt the beginnings of a headache behind her eyes. She wasn't sure if she should go inside again and find someone to help her, or if there would be anyone there. Then she remembered—Rafe was around. No, she wasn't going back inside.

She sat forward and pushed the button again. This time, loud static came over the speaker, then a voice. "Security."

"I'm in the parking lot and I need to get out. The gate's shut."

"Name?"

If he had a list, she wasn't on it. But she gave it a shot. "Megan Gallagher. I just started today and—"

"I know," the voice said, and she realized it was Rafe.

The next instant the gate slowly rose. "Thank you," she called into the speaker, but there was no response.

He probably hadn't heard her. She rolled up the window and eased out onto the street, then stopped by the curb, aware of the gate going down behind her as she reached for the paper with the directions. Mr. Lawrence had made them simple, even writing down the estimated distance between turns.

She started off, and as she got closer, recognized the area. It's where she'd thought the loft would be, right in the middle of a redevelopment zone. It could be just fine. It might be nice now, and not dangerous. It could have upscale residences and elegant businesses. The loft might be like the ones she'd seen in New York when she'd visited Quint. She remembered him telling her some of the prices and they were outrageous. People actually had bidding wars, driving prices through the ceiling, all wanting to live in such places. Maybe that's the way it was with the LynTech loft.

She spotted the street she was looking for, turned onto it and knew she was wrong. It was lined with warehouses, half of them boarded up, the others with stark security lights on them. Interspersed were other, smaller buildings, some abandoned, none remotely like the elegant renovated places she'd hoped for. She drove slowly, noticing that there were no people on the street, and just a scattering of cars parked by the curb. Streetlamps provided a little light, at least the ones with bulbs not broken, but there were no garages in sight, no driveways, and no parking stalls.

Megan spotted the number she was looking for halfway down the block on the right, and pulled her car to the curb in front of an old van that looked as if a hippie probably lived in it. Ahead, three motorcycles were parked, nose in, in front of the two-story warehouse, whose only ornamentation were two potted plants sitting on either side of a steel security door. At least there was light from a caged fixture over the entry.

She turned off the car, double-checked the address, then took several deep breaths. She could barely admit it to herself, but what Rafe Diaz had said had scared her more than a little. If he'd intended to do that, he'd succeeded.

She picked up the keys, gripping the one tagged for the front door, then pushed everything else into her briefcase and got out of the car, leaving the boxes for later. Locking the door, Megan set the alarm and practically ran around the vehicle and across the cement sidewalk to the warehouse entrance.

She pushed the key in the lock, turned it and heard a click, then opened the door. She went inside, closed it behind her and stood for a moment in the barren-looking foyer. Two doors, one to the right and one dead ahead, came off of it, and to her left was an old service elevator. The note had said the loft was on the second floor, straight across from the lift. She stepped forward and raised the chain gate on the elevator, then got in, relieved when it began to move.

Reaching the second level, she went to the door directly across the hallway and got out the second key. But before she could put it in the lock, another door off the hallway to her right opened and a mountain of a man stepped out. He had on a leather vest over a massive bare chest, plus faded Levi's, heavy motorcycle boots, and a skullcap over long gray hair, which was pulled back in a ponytail. There were tattoos on each of his massive biceps and one visible through the open front of the vest. She thought she could make out *Die* as one of the words.

Megan didn't move, not even able to push the key into the lock. She just stared at him as he came closer, shocked that the floor didn't vibrate each time his big feet hit it. "You got a problem, lady?" he asked in a voice that matched his size.

"No, no, no," she managed to reply, and knew that he had to own one of the three bikes downstairs. That meant there were two more like him somewhere around. "I just...I came here...and I was going inside."

He frowned at her. "I was told that place was empty."

"I'm just here for a few weeks. I'm with Lyn-Tech."

He eyed her up and down, then actually smiled at her, showing surprisingly white, even teeth. "Well, no offense, but you hardly look like one of those big executives over there at LynTech."

"I'm an attorney."

He glanced at the briefcase she was clutching tightly, as if the supple leather could protect her. "Need any help?"

"No, but thank you very much for offering," she said quickly.

"Well, I'm just next door kicking back, but we'll try to keep the noise down for you, Miss...?"

"Gallagher," she said. "Megan Gallagher."

"Trig," he said, offering no other name but that. "Now remember, if you need anything, just come on over, or throw a rock at the fire escape window, you hear?"

"Yes...thank you," she said.

With that he turned and headed back to his loft. But at the door he hesitated, then looked at her over his shoulder, smiling again. "If I ever need a good attorney, I'll be calling on you, okay?"

She tried to smile and nod, then he was gone, the door closing behind him, and she exhaled in a rush that left her vaguely light-headed. Quickly, she pushed the key in the lock, and when the door swung back, she all but dove into the shadows within. She closed the door, fumbled with the lock, then stood very still. She'd made it.

Exhaling with relief, she reached to the right of the door and found a light switch. Two lamps came on, illuminating the space. She glanced around, at high, shadow-filled ceilings lined with criss-crossed pipes and duct work. The space right in front of her was a sitting area, with two sofas, a chair, tables and a TV on the wall to the right. At the back she saw high louvered windows that ran the width of the loft.

The cavernous space was divided by walls that reached only two-thirds of the way to the twelve-foot ceiling, and from what little she could see, there were two other "rooms" to the left. She stepped farther inside and saw a work area directly under the back windows, with louvered ones over them, framed by long, low windows on either side. *The fire escape exit,* she thought, but knew she wouldn't be going out there to throw rocks at Trig's window.

She put her briefcase on one lamp table, then went back to the work area, snapped on a side lamp and saw a full office set up—everything from a computer to a fax machine, to a scanner and two phones. Mr. Lawrence had been right about this place—that it could serve as her office when she couldn't get to LynTech.

A shrill ringing startled her, and she looked at the phones. One of them had a flashing light at the base, and she picked up the cordless receiver. The LED screen was lit, and showed the message Unknown Caller. She realized that Mr. Lawrence was the only person who would be calling her here, so she hit the Talk button and said, "Hello?"

"You got inside okay?"

She couldn't believe the voice coming over the line, and thought for a minute she'd imagined it. "Who is this?" she asked.

"Rafe Diaz. I was just checking to make sure everything was okay."

She felt tension at the back of her neck, and the headache was becoming a reality. "Excuse me? You're checking on me?"

"I was thinking about that area, and thought it might be a good idea to make sure you got inside okay."

"Why?" She asked the question more abruptly then she'd meant to, unnerved that she remembered clearly that look of concern in his eyes in the garage, right before she'd offended him. He'd been angry, but now he was checking to make sure she was okay. His call and concern touched her.

"It's my job."

"Maybe you should check that job description," she said.

"I'm probably being overzealous, and you're probably just fine, so I'll—"

She didn't hear the rest, because right then something flew at her, hitting her hard in the right shoulder, sending her reeling sideways. The phone shot out of her hand, and the next thing she knew, she'd hit the floor, landing on her left side and wincing in pain. She instinctively pushed herself up off the floor to her feet, still wondering what had hit her so hard to make her fall.

She grabbed the edge of the desk and frantically looked around. Her heart hammered against her ribs, and she could barely breathe. There was nothing but shadows and silence around her now, however. She saw the phone on the floor and quickly picked it up, gasping into the receiver, "Rafe? Rafe?"

Nothing. She hit the Disconnect button frantically, but there wasn't even a dial tone now. And standing there in the light, she suddenly felt like a target for anyone who might also be in the loft. She dropped the phone on the table, then eased to her left, into shadows for protection, and stood very still. She couldn't hear anything at all beyond her own ragged breathing, and couldn't see anything outside the glow of the lamps.

She glanced at the door. It was twenty, maybe thirty feet away, and if she ran, she could reach it and slip out in mere seconds. She could make her escape and call the police from her cell phone. The only thing wrong with that scenario was that her phone wasn't in her pocket any longer. She'd put it in her briefcase before she'd come up here. And her briefcase was on the lamp table by the sofa. She could grab the whole briefcase as she ran toward the door. She could even use it as a weapon if she had to.

She got ready, then ran as fast as she could to the sofa, all the while expecting someone to leap out and tackle her before she got what she needed. But she made it to the table, grabbed for her briefcase and accidentally sent the lamp flying to the floor in the process. It crashed, shattering on the wooden floors. She ignored the sound and kept running for the door. She grasped the knob, turned it and pulled, but the door didn't open.

The lock. She flipped it open and tried again, but the door still wouldn't budge. She looked up and down the frame, then saw a lock near the top that must have automatically clicked into place when she came in. She reached up, turned the lever, heard it snap back, and was about to pull the door open when someone pounded loudly on the outside.

Megan jerked back as if she'd been scalded, and had a truly paranoid flash of being attacked from all sides. She stared at the door, unable to say or do anything until a deep, muffled voice called out, "Open the door! Open up!"

She flinched at the sound, then managed to find her own voice. "Who...who's there?" she called back.

"It's Rafe Diaz! Open up!"

Chapter Four

Megan stared at the door, not believing her ears, and didn't move until he called again. "Megan, open up!"

Rafe? She went closer, reaching for the doorknob, but hesitated, afraid of what she'd find. "Rafe?" she managed to call through the door.

"It's me. Open up!"

She twisted the knob and jerked the door back, and discovered it was him. The instant she saw him, she ran into his arms and held on to him for dear life. "Thank goodness it's you," she gasped against the heat and strength of his chest.

"It's me," he said in a whispered voice that rumbled in her ears. Then his arms tightened around her and closed out the fear. "I'm here. It's okay. Just tell me what happened."

She held him for another heartbeat, letting a sense of safety filter into her being. It was okay. She was safe, safer than she'd ever felt in her life. Then she realized who was holding her, who she'd made her anchor, and she eased back from him. Wrong. *Really wrong,* she thought, but couldn't make herself totally let go of him. "Someone...someone's in there. They h-hit me, and I..."

Before she could finish, he was pushing her down the hallway, getting between her and the open loft door. Then he had his gun out, ready, and he said, "Get on your phone and call 911."

Her phone? "It's in my briefcase, inside."

"Just go and find a phone. Knock on doors, anything, but get the cops up here," he said, then literally pushed her toward the elevator.

She stopped when she reached it, but couldn't make herself get in. Instead, she turned just in time to see Rafe slip into the loft and out of sight. There was silence, nothing, and she found herself slowly going back to the open door. She cautiously peered inside, but saw only darkness. No sounds. No movement. It was as if Rafe had vanished.

She looked down the hallway to Trig's loft. She could get him. He was bigger than anyone she'd ever seen. And she started to turn, but stopped dead when she heard something from inside her loft. A thud, another thud, then a scuffling sound. Raw fear shot through her, and she screamed, "Rafe!" and ran toward the sounds, but didn't get very far.

She literally ran right into Rafe as he came toward her out of the side room. He had her again in his arms, but this time he'd been the one to reach out to catch her, to hold her against him and keep her from falling. The hug was fierce, intense, then he whispered hoarsely, "I told you to go, to get help." And she felt every word shudder along the length of her body pressed against his. "I told you to go."

"I heard...I thought..." She bit her lip. There was no way she could tell him how afraid she'd been or why she'd come in when she heard the noises. No way at all.

"No, you *didn't* think," he practically growled, and eased her away from him, though he kept a tight hold on her upper arms. "You didn't leave."

She stood there, enduring the connection, then did something she seldom did. She apologized. "I'm sorry," she whispered. "I'm so sorry."

She felt the tension in him, the unsteadiness, and saw fear in his eyes. Then, without warning, he leaned closer, kissed her quickly and fiercely, and the fear was gone. Megan was left wondering if she'd imagined it or if it had been real. She was free and standing on her own in the loft, with a good two feet of space between herself and Rafe.

Nothing made sense to her, and she couldn't even get out the words to ask him what had just happened and why. She saw him close his eyes, take a deep breath and release it, then he was looking at her again. "You're so damn infuriating," he muttered through clenched teeth.

She tried to come up with some way to make sense of all that had happened since Rafe Diaz walked up to her the night at the ball, and couldn't. Her mind refused to focus on what he was or wasn't, except that he was married. "Sorry," she heard herself saying, a stupid response when all she wanted to do was demand to know why he'd just kissed her.

"So you've said." He ran a hand roughly over his face, and his wedding band gleamed.

She swallowed hard, then looked down and saw that his gun was holstered at his hip.

"You—you didn't have to...hurt anyone, did you?"

"I tried, but he was too fast for me."

She felt the blood drain from her face. "Oh, my God," she breathed. "There was someone...?"

"Some *thing,*" he said, and motioned to the partial wall of the room he'd just left moments ago. "There's the culprit."

She didn't understand what he was talking about until her gaze followed the direction he indicated, at the top of the partition. Then she saw her attacker. A huge orange cat was perched calmly on the ledge there, a massive ball of fur with dark eyes watching them inscrutably. "A cat?" Megan's relief was overwhelming.

"You're damn lucky it was just a cat," he muttered. "If it had been—"

She turned on Rafe, her nerves frayed beyond measure. "Okay, I didn't go to the next-door neighbor, who happens to be a biker the size of the state of Texas, and I came back in here. It's okay. Nothing happened. It's a cat. Even I can deal with a cat."

He unexpectedly reached out and cupped her chin, making her keep their eye contact. "But it could have been someone the size of Texas in here," he muttered.

They should both be laughing at the way she'd overreacted to a cat attacking her. They should maybe be having a drink and rehashing how foolish she'd been, how it would make a good story when they told it to others. They definitely shouldn't be inches from each other, with him still angry at her, and her so confused by everything that her headache was coming back full force.

"Well, I'm glad it's just a cat," she said, and looked at the animal. The cat calmly licked one paw, then proceeded to clean his face, all the while staring at the two humans below. "How did he get in here?"

"There's an open window," Rafe said.

She looked at the windows and saw what he meant—open louvers over what she thought was the fire escape window. "He got in through there, but jumped at me from behind when I was over by the computer."

"Looks like he comes and goes as he pleases. You probably intruded on his privacy. He was startled, tried to get away, maybe to get to the window, and hit you."

It made sense to her, but that was about the only thing that did at that moment. She turned, looking past Rafe to the still-open door, then the broken lamp on the floor. She moved away, going to the lamp and picking up the pieces.

"He did that, too?" Rafe asked from behind her.

"No, I did it trying to grab my briefcase and get out of here." She looked at the cracked lamp base and the dented shade, then put them back on the table. "It's ruined," she said.

"You're lucky that's the only casualty," he said from right behind her.

She spun around. "Just stop. You've tried to scare me about everything to do with this place, and I've had enough."

"I'm out of here," he muttered, and started for the door.

But before he got to the exit, she realized something. "What are you even doing here?"

He stopped and spoke without turning. "You screamed on the phone, then it went dead. I came over to make sure you were okay." She didn't remember screaming, but she probably had. "I thought you were calling from LynTech, then you showed up on my doorstep." Another thing hit her. "And you got through the security door."

He stood still for a moment, then turned back to her. "I was going past and saw your car, and thought I'd call up to make sure you got in safely. Then you screamed and…" He tugged at the tie of his uniform, unfurling it, then undid the top button of his shirt. "The security door—and I use that term loosely—opened when that big biker you were talking about came out. Seeing my uniform, he actually held the door for me."

She heard what he said about the door, about Trig actually letting him in, but she was still hung up on one of the first things he'd stated. "You were going past this place?"

The last few minutes blurred together for Rafe, melding the shock, the fear and the feeling of Megan shaking in his arms. He tried to separate everything, to focus, but all he could remember was her scream, then being here and thinking that she was in real danger. The raw terror that surged through him, the suffocating need to save her, the fear that he would be too late… Then going inside, finding the cat, letting himself breathe again, only to discover Megan back in the loft without going for help…

It was like reliving a nightmare, that horrible feeling of doing everything he could, and it not being enough. The feeling of helplessly watching a horror, and having no ability to protect anyone. He hadn't been there with Gabriella, hadn't been able to tell her to get out, to run. But he knew that she hadn't run. She'd never had a chance. But Megan had. Damn it, she'd had the chance but hadn't taken it.

He exhaled harshly. "You know, you could thank me, instead of putting me through twenty questions." He heard the tension in his voice and knew it was time he left. Before he did something he'd regret. "And the next time someone tells you to get help, do it."

He turned; the door was right there. But she spoke and it stopped him again. "It was a cat," Megan repeated.

Yes, it had been a cat. He turned back to her and watched her lift her chin slightly.

"We both overreacted," she added. That was when her tongue touched her lips, a fleeting action, but enough to make his world start to tip again.

Overreacted? He'd kissed her. He didn't know why. Out of anger? Frustration? Need? "And you're damn lucky that's all it was," he countered.

"You know, it's your fault," she said out of the blue.

Just when he thought he had her figured out, she pulled something like this. "*My* fault?"

"Sure. If you hadn't scared me about being in this area, I never would have reacted the way I did."

"Why didn't I think of that?" he said sardonically, focusing on the fact that she probably never took the blame for anything. "That's brilliant, Counselor. It's my fault." He'd left his hat in the car. Otherwise, he would have saluted her and left. As it was, he did the next best thing. He simply said, "And now I'm really out of here."

He turned again and stepped through the door, but she wasn't letting him off that easily. "I'd really stop and check your job description sometime if I were you," she called after him.

Against his better judgment, he turned again. She was still by the sofa, an aloof, sarcastic woman who bore little resemblance to the one who had run into his arms for protection. He found sarcasm to match hers. "Are you always this rude, or did you go to some private school to teach you how to do it properly?"

"Are you this obnoxious naturally, or were you self-taught?" she countered.

He stared at her long and hard, thankful that his emotions at that point were clear cut: anger. Then she crossed her arms on her breasts and the diamond on her finger flashed in the light. "Heaven help your fiancé," he muttered, then strode across the hallway to the lift.

He was inside, turning to pull down the chain-link door, when he saw her again. She was standing in the doorway, one hand on the jamb, leaning out toward him. "You...you're married. Does your wife know what you do on your way home?" The next instant, the door slammed shut and what should have been relief only shook him more.

His wife. He jerked down the barrier and jabbed at the Down button. He uttered a raw expletive, braced for the searing pain that always came with those words...*his wife.* But all that followed was anger. Searing anger. Anger at Megan, and anger at himself for ever calling her in the first place. He could be home with the boys, and Megan Gallagher wouldn't be part of any equation. But he wasn't home. Instead he was here, getting out of the elevator and heading for the exit.

He was raging at himself as he went out into the balmy night and toward his car, feeling as if he'd been hit in the gut by an iron fist. He had no idea why he'd driven by the loft, let alone called up there to check on Megan. He'd been heading home, but found himself going in the wrong direction. Then he'd looked up and noticed he was passing the address he'd seen on the letter from Wayne Lawrence. He'd spotted her car parked between heavy-duty motorcycles and a hippie van. Instead of just driving past, the way he should have, he'd pulled to the curb beyond the bikes, then used his cell phone to call Zane, and in two minutes he'd had the phone number for the loft and had called it. Then he'd heard the scream.

He crossed to his SUV, parked in front of the bikes, got in and started it up with a roar. A cat had attacked her? He drove off with a squeal of tires. Hell, if he was a cat he'd probably attack her, too. Right now she had likely forgotten how foolishly she'd acted, and was worried about cat hairs on her clothes.

His cell phone rang, and he took it out with a glance at the LED readout. Zane's home number. "Zane?"

"Yeah, it's me."

"What's up?" he asked as he forced himself to slow the car and drive in the right direction toward home. Hopefully by the time he got to the boys, he'd be calmer.

"You hung up so fast when you called, I forgot to ask why you needed the phone number at the loft."

He thought about lying, just saying it was for his own reference, but the last person he'd lie to was Zane. "I found someone in Legal going through Mr. Lawrence's desk when I made my rounds tonight."

"You what?"

"It was a false alarm," he said. "She's the lady I told you about, the one I thought was crashing the ball. The one meeting up with Wayne Lawrence."

"What was she doing there? Waiting for him?"

"No, going through his desk."

"What the hell?"

"Yeah, it got my attention, too. But it turned out she's new, and she wasn't on the list yet. She's working in Legal with Mr. Lawrence."

"Jack Ford mentioned something about Mr. Lawrence getting someone from our West Coast office to fill a temporary vacancy in the company. Why in hell was she going through the guy's desk?"

"She was getting something that she'd left in his office earlier. It turned out it wasn't anything subversive."

"That's a relief. But what does this have to do with you needing the phone number for the loft?"

"That's where Lawrence is putting her up. I haven't been in the area for a long time, and last time I looked, it was pretty rough.'' He glanced out the window, at a neighborhood that was still iffy, but heading in the right direction. ''I went past it on my way home, and thought I'd check to make sure she got in safely.''

''On your way home?''

''Okay, I made a wrong turn.'' That was so true it hurt. ''And I thought, since I was there, it wouldn't hurt to check.''

''Lindsey lived there when I met her, and Jack's lived there. In fact, LynTech is in the process of buying the building from the owner, Jack's new father-in-law, George Armstrong, one of the last hippies around and one of the biggest LynTech stockholders.''

The hippie van. That explained that, at least. ''It doesn't look too bad, actually.''

''I take it everything's okay?''

''It is now. When we were on the phone, she screamed and the line went dead. Seems some huge orange cat got in and scared her to death.''

Zane laughed out loud, then finally said, ''That's Joey. Someone should have warned her, I guess. He came with the loft, and we tried to bring him over here, but he runs away, and always shows up back there. I'll have to tell Lindsey that he made it back again. He's been gone for four days.''

''He's there, big, fat and scary.''

''A perfect description,'' Zane said with a chuckle. ''I need to get going, but wanted to make sure everything was okay.''

''Sure, everything's fine,'' he replied, the lie almost sticking in his throat. ''Just fine.''

''See you tomorrow,'' Zane said, and hung up.

Rafe tossed the cell phone onto the seat and gripped the steering wheel with both hands. ''Fine,'' he said again, just to hear the word and willing it to be so. It wasn't, but he'd keep saying it, hoping that somewhere down the line, he might wake up one morning and things would be fine.

By the time Rafe got home the boys were asleep and Carmella was ready to leave. She'd jumped at the chance to come to Houston so she could spend time with her sister. ''A paid vacation,'' she'd told him with delight. She'd been with the boys since they were born. She was a short, kind woman who had raised her own children, and now she was helping to raise his.

She'd spent the day with the boys, getting them ready for the day care center tomorrow, explaining, as Rafe had instructed her, that they would be called Diaz. It was a game for them, and they'd fallen into it easily. They were excited about going to the center, about the game and being near Rafe. That was a relief. Rafe walked her out to her car so she could go to her sister's, and waited until she was heading through the gates at the end of the driveway before he turned and went back inside the adobe ranch house.

As soon as he closed the door, he started his routine, checking all the windows, all the doors, locking everything, then finally setting the alarm system he'd had upgraded the day he arrived. Compulsive, some called him, obsessed with the ritual, but he needed to do it. Needed to know his home was secure.

He walked back through the darkened house, which was spread out on one level in a long U, with Spanish tile everywhere. The ranch house sat on a ten-acre property, with lots of room for the boys to run and play and have their dogs and horses. They'd never lived here before, and he'd only used it occasionally, when he had to be in the area. He'd bought it as a tax write-off, but now that he was here, he found he liked that it didn't have a lot of memories built into it.

He checked on Gabe and Greg in their bedroom, and found them in the same bed, the second one barely mussed. They were snuggled up together, sound asleep. He stared down at them, and could almost hear Gabriella saying they were his boys, looked just like him. He thought they looked like themselves. He pulled the covers up over them, kissed them both, neither of them stirring.

He crossed and checked the windows, then finally went into the master bedroom right across the hall from them and flipped on the lights. The first thing he saw was the massive king-size bed on the wall opposite the French doors. It was made of heavy, rough-hewn timbers, dark and impressive, and looked very empty at that moment. He turned away, stripped off his uniform, socks and underwear, put his gun in the lockbox in the closet, then crossed to the door that looked out onto the terrace. He turned off the alarm for the doors, then went out naked into the softness of the night.

Eschewing the pool beyond the security fence straight ahead, where he swam laps, he opted for the hot tub on the terrace. He slipped into the warm water, sank down and rested his head on the back support, staring up at the starlit sky. He let the heat seep into his body, willing himself to relax, but it didn't happen. He couldn't shut off his mind, and no matter what he did to reroute his thoughts, he kept reliving that rush up to the loft, Megan throwing herself into his arms, and his raw fear for her.

He closed his eyes, but the images played out, anyway. Megan looking up at him, Rafe trying to get her out of the loft to protect her, then seeing her there again, right in the line of danger. And his rage, his relief, his needs…

Rafe opened his eyes quickly. Needs? That didn't fit into this at all. No more than him kissing her, needing to feel the reality of her against his lips. Her parting shot still rang in his ears. She thought he was married and fooling around. Coming on to her. He actually preferred her to think that. He didn't want her sympathy, or her saying anything like Francine had, about ''passing'' or ''losing.''

''Heaven help me,'' he breathed, a bit taken aback that her words hadn't brought blinding pain, just anger. That coolness that returned, the way she set her boundaries, the way she dismissed him when she didn't need him… Boundaries weren't bad, he'd admit that, and they were probably a good thing with a woman like Megan. But he was the one who would set them. Not a woman who looked down on him for being an hourly worker, not worth very much.

He pushed himself up and out of the tub, then padded dripping wet back into the bedroom, closed the doors, reset the alarm, and went to find a towel in the bathroom. After he put on his shorts, he stretched out on the empty bed and stared up at the shadows on the ceiling.

His stomach was still knotted and he felt a restlessness that he knew would keep sleep at bay. There had been so many nights he'd struggled to get through. Sleep often eluded him, and even when it didn't, it wasn't a peaceful rest. He'd awake tired in the morning, due to sadness, grief and guilt. Tonight was different.

Tonight he felt so very alone, and before he knew what he was doing, he was counting each breath he took, remembering Megan's words. *You're married. Does your wife know what you do on your way home?*

He shifted, rested his hands on his stomach and felt his wedding ring. His fingers touched it, caressing the plain gold band. "Let go," he'd been told, so often he'd lost count. "It wasn't your fault." He pressed his right hand over his left and closed his eyes. "Let go."

The instant he shut his eyes, an image came to him, with such a jolt that he bolted upright in bed. But it wasn't from his past, those images that had haunted him for almost two years. Instead the vision that came with aching clarity was of Megan Gallagher. Even sitting in the middle of the bed with his eyes wide open now, he could see her. Glancing at him from under her lashes. The fullness of her lips. The curve of her hips and the softness of her skin...

He got up, but even standing on the cold tiles, he couldn't stop his body from responding to the images, driven as he was by insane thoughts that he couldn't let himself think. He pushed them away, banishing them. He'd never been a man driven by sex. He'd loved it, and it had been a marvelous part of what he'd had before. He wasn't stupid enough to believe the urges were gone forever. But he'd be damned if he'd let a woman like Megan Gallagher evoke anything like that in him. He wouldn't let her bring out any feeling that he could protect her. He couldn't and wouldn't ever try that again.

He crossed the room to a built-in entertainment center, found a DVD and started it before returning to bed. He crushed the pillows behind his head and stared determinedly at the big-screen TV as the movie's opening credits rolled past.

"Are you always this pushy and annoying?"

He stared at the screen, trying to push away Megan's words, and his response to it. *"Heaven help your fiancé."*

"Pity the poor fool," he muttered then, clasping his hands behind his head as he watched the images flashing on the television screen. Pity the man who had to deal with her attitudes and her snobbery. And the man who endured her condescension and barbs. The same man who would reach out in the night for her, feel her with his hands and make her smile.

MEGAN DIDN'T GET TO BED until the wee hours of the morning, partly because she'd been going over the incorporation papers for the day care center she'd had in her briefcase, and partly because the cat unnerved her with the way it sat on the high walls, staring unblinkingly at her. Another part of her kept going over what had happened with Rafe.

She finally gave up working, tired of having her

mind going in ten directions at once. She glanced at the telephone, truly tempted to call Ryan, just to hear his voice and remind herself what her reality was. But she couldn't. It was the middle of the night, and she really should just go to bed.

The cat was still on the ledge, and she was going to leave him there forever if she had to, but the minute she started for the bedroom, he meowed. It didn't take an animal psychic to know he wanted something, and from her experience with the wild cats on the ranch, the one thing they all wanted was food. She went into the small kitchen, found a couple of cans of tuna in the nearly bare cupboards and opened one for him.

She put the food on a plate, laid it on the floor, then stood back and talked to the animal. "There's your food. Eat and leave."

His tail swished, and his eyes narrowed.

"And the window's going to be closed the minute your tail goes through," she muttered, heading for the bedroom again. She looked back when she got to the entry, just in time to see the cat leap gracefully to the floor and cast her one decidedly haughty look before starting to eat.

She left him to his tuna and went into the bedroom, a fairly stark room with a large bed angled toward the high windows, a dresser, a couple of nightstands with lamps sitting on them. She was a bit taken aback when she lifted her luggage by the dresser and found it was empty. Whoever had brought her things from the hotel had also unpacked for her. She found her nightshirt, a well-worn T-shirt from college that she truly wished a stranger hadn't seen, folded neatly in the top drawer.

She grabbed it and went into the bathroom, only to find all of her makeup and toiletries laid out near the sink.

She tugged at the shower curtain on the ring over the tub, turned on the water, then stripped off her clothes. It felt glorious to step under the spray of warm water.

She found body wash and smoothed it over her arms and shoulders, then closed her eyes as a fantasy sprang to life. She never had fantasies, but this burst on her, fully formed and riveting. She could almost hear someone whisper her name, the sound coming to her in the steamy heat surrounding her.

Someone coming up to the curtain, parting it behind her, then slipping inside. His arms would come around her waist, pulling her back against him, his body molding to hers. His lips would find the nape of her neck, his hands slipping to her stomach, keeping her against him. Moving sinuously, he would whisper in her ear, his hands cupping her breasts, making her moan softly.

She'd turn, circling her arms around his neck, lifting her face to his, and… She literally gasped at the image she'd brought to life in her mind. Her fantasy lover. He wasn't Ryan. He had midnight-dark eyes, black hair, a sleek body, deeply tanned, and a wedding band on his left hand.

Chapter Five

Megan opened her eyes quickly, scanning the empty spaces around her. Steam rose in the air, and her hands were pressed to her stomach. She took a deep, gulping breath and reached blindly for the faucet to turn off the water, then stepped out of the shower onto the cold floor. Grabbing a towel, she scrubbed at her skin, trying to rub away the sensation of Rafe's hands on her. She was tired and crazy from the pressures of this trip, the engagement, everything. And Rafe Diaz had been thrown into the mix—where he didn't belong.

She tossed the towel over the sink, slipped on her T-shirt and hurried into the bedroom. She'd taken two steps before her foot hit something that hissed and squealed on impact, and as Megan screamed, it darted off into the shadows.

"You damn cat!" she called after him, and heard something thud to the floor. She hurried to the main room, turned on the nearest lamp and saw the tail of the cat disappearing through the open transom window. On the floor by the computer was her briefcase. He'd knocked it off the table while making his escape.

She looked at the window and for a moment thought of climbing on the worktable to close it. Then she decided she wouldn't bother. Instead she crossed to the bed, climbed into it and settled into the soft linen.

She curled onto her side and cautiously closed her eyes. But there were no surprises, no man with dark eyes, and she sighed with relief.

MEGAN WAS JERKED out of sleep suddenly, and looked up at the wall by the door, the place the cat had been each morning for the past three days. Sure enough, he was there. In the filtered light of early morning she saw him staring down at her, his tail twitching from side to side. She considered rolling over and trying to go back to sleep, but didn't bother. She knew he'd start to meow if she ignored him.

She got out of bed and went into the kitchen to give him the last of the tuna. According to the call she'd received from Lindsey Holden, the cat's name was Joey, he loved the loft and she'd have food delivered. "Just let him hang out there," Lindsey had told her. "I'll try to figure out what to do about him later." So Joey hung out, got fed, kept his distance and stared at Megan for what seemed hours while she worked.

She left the food for him this morning, and the ritual began. He slowly walked along the tops of the partial walls, waited for her to get a good distance from the food, then he gracefully jumped to the floor. He checked on her again to make sure she was leaving, then he began to eat.

She'd never had an affinity for animals when she was a child on the ranch, no more than she'd had an affinity for playing with dolls or rescuing wounded birds. She'd never liked getting dirty, and she would have rather read than do anything else. And this cat was just plain annoying at best, but she'd let him hang out.

She went back into the bedroom and automatically crossed to the bathroom. But as she had for three mornings, she hesitated before taking a shower then finally did so as quickly as she could—in and out. It was simple. No time for any weird thoughts or fantasies. Then she dressed in pale beige slacks, nipped in at the waist with a narrow gold belt, along with a soft, silky green shirt with cap sleeves, and low heels. She brushed her hair up into a twist, and with just a hint of lipstick, she was done—at barely seven o'clock.

She'd been told to be in at nine o'clock, so it was far too early to head into the office, and far too early to wake Ryan up with a phone call. They had a routine. She called him at nine in the morning, her time. If she didn't reach him, he'd call her in the evening. So she settled at the workstation with a cup of hot water and the last envelope of instant coffee she found in the kitchen, then worked on the figures Mr. Lawrence had given her of the funds raised at the ball. She didn't know where the cat had gone, but by the time she looked up, he'd disappeared and the clock read eight-thirty.

She got her things together, put on her earpiece and slipped her cell phone into her breast pocket, then decided to try Ryan early. She hit the Connect button. ''Ryan. Home,'' she said, and waited to be connected as she opened the loft door and looked out into the hallway.

"Connecting Ryan. Home," the computer voice said in her ear as she scanned the hallway, thankfully finding no huge biker or a security guard out to save the world. No, the biker was probably still asleep after the party she'd heard going on next door last night, and the guard was probably where he'd been for the past three mornings—at home with his wife and a bunch of kids, sitting around a huge table for breakfast.

She hadn't seen Rafe again at LynTech and again assumed he worked nights. That was okay. In fact, it was perfect. She didn't want to see him.

By the time she got to the first floor, Ryan's answering machine had picked up and hung up. Then she went out into a clear, warm day with only a hint of the humidity that she knew was going to come later. Her car was still there, untouched, and had been each day, despite Rafe's ominous warnings. She was surprised to see Trig's motorcycle and the other two bikes gone. They must have taken the party to a new location, she thought.

She drove through the morning rush hour traffic that clogged the downtown streets, and as she did she found herself looking for a large black SUV, the way she had every other morning. Rafe had said he was "passing by," so she assumed he lived around here somewhere with his wife and family. But the more she saw of the neighborhood in daylight, coming and going, the more she knew he couldn't have been going by her place on his way home. What housing there was in the refurbished area would be costly, and even the loft she was in didn't come cheap.

But if he hadn't been on his way home, what was he up to? A married man looking for something outside of the marriage? That brought a sick feeling to the back of her throat. It seemed better to think that maybe he hadn't believed her reason for being in Mr. Lawrence's office. She'd heard that security had been beefed up recently, but no one she'd talked to seemed to know why. Just that they were "tightening" things as a precaution. And Rafe was definitely taking that seriously.

She pulled into the LynTech garage behind two other cars, parked and turned off the car. Then she put in another call to Ryan. She just wanted to hear his voice, to think sane thoughts again. But the answering machine picked up once more, so she left a message, and said they could talk that evening. As she got out of her car and went inside, heading toward the elevators, Megan wondered where Ryan was and why he wasn't there to receive her usual morning call. When she stepped off the elevator, the receptionist, Ellen, was in her usual place, behind the desk.

When she saw Megan, she waved to her. "Megan, just a minute?"

The woman was a gossip, and Megan didn't have the time or stomach to listen to speculations about the newest couple on the block, or who was getting a divorce. But she made herself smile and cross to the desk. "Good morning."

Ellen had hair so blond it looked silver, and she wore too much makeup. But she was pleasant enough and smiling. She picked up a folder and leaned across the desk to offer it to Megan. "Mr. Lawrence left this for you. He wants you to go down to the day care center and speak to Mrs. Garner right away."

"Oh, okay," Megan said, shifting her briefcase to her other hand to take the folder and glance at it. "Mary Garner" was written in the top right corner. She hadn't met Mary Garner yet, but Ellen had spoken about the woman a couple of days ago.

"Mary Garner and our Mr. Lewis, the founder of this whole company are…well, what you'd call good friends." She'd lifted one eyebrow slightly. "If you get my drift."

Megan made a mental note right then not to share any gossip with this woman for any reason. "It's on the lobby level, isn't it?"

"You bet. Back down the elevator, ground floor, bright doors with the sign 'Just For Kids' on them."

"Okay, I'll just put my things in my office and—"

"I wouldn't take too much time," Ellen said quickly. "Mrs. Garner's waiting and, as I told you before, she and Mr. Lewis…" She held up her hand, crossing her middle finger tightly over her forefinger, and all but whispered, "She's got important friends, and Mr. Lawrence said she needed you down there as soon as you arrived."

"Okay, I'll head right down."

"You just watch when you meet Mary, and—"

Megan was saved by the ringing of the phone. "Catch you later," Ellen said just before she answered the call with polite formality. "LynTech Legal. How may I direct your call?"

Megan went back to the elevators and headed down to the day care center. She glanced at her watch: nine o'clock exactly. She stepped out at the lobby level, spotted the doors to the center and caught a flash of movement to her right. She glanced that way and saw a security guard alongside a businessman in a tailored suit. The man looked like Zane Holden, although she hadn't formally met him, only talked to his wife, and the guard was Rafe. She didn't have any doubt. He walked quickly down the hall with Holden, then they both disappeared into a side corridor.

She'd thought he was on nights. Wrong. She'd thought if or when she saw him again she'd just walk past and not give him a second glance. Not this time. She took a deep breath, exhaled, then crossed to the brightly colored doors directly in front of her.

RAFE HAD ALMOST RUN INTO Zane when he left the center after checking on the boys. His friend had glanced at him, and for a moment Rafe was certain Zane didn't recognize him. Then he realized he was in a rush and looking worried. But as soon as he realized it was Rafe, they'd left the center together, headed down a back hallway and veered off into a side hall that led to maintenance storage rooms.

Zane stopped and turned to face Rafe. "There's trouble."

"What kind of trouble?"

His expression was grim. "Another leak." He handed Rafe a newspaper he'd had under his arm.

Rafe scanned the main article above the fold in the business section of the daily. He spotted the LynTech name right away, and read about the very successful merger with EJS Corporation and LynTech, a done deal. But the next line stopped him: "With LynTech in the catbird seat with this prime acquisition, they are in a position of power to take down the Andress Group, a rumored target of theirs. Their sights are set and…"

Rafe looked up at Zane, who was watching him intently. "Is it true that you're going after Andress?"

"Not now, but we thought about it and decided that it was too top-heavy in research to justify it." He hit the paper with the tip of his finger. "But *if* we were going after it, it would be a dead deal now."

"Who knew?" Rafe asked.

"Me, Matt, Jack and Robert Lewis," Zane said, naming his co-CEO and another top level employee, as well as LynTech's founder. "Robert had done business with Andress before he stepped down, and he had some good input. In fact, he was the one who pointed out the flaws in the idea."

"Then this won't hurt you?"

"Not now. Not this time." Zane raked his fingers through his sandy hair. "But the next time…" He shrugged. "Business is rough right now, and this only makes it rougher."

"If only the people you listed knew about it, that makes the leak unlikely to have come from the top."

Zane frowned. "There were a few others."

"Who?"

"Mr. Lawrence in Legal. He did some background work on the idea before we decided to tank it."

That pricked Rafe's interest. "Did he do the work himself?"

"I don't know. I'd assume that he'd delegate with discretion."

"Can you find out who he used?"

"Sure. Any ideas?"

"No." Rafe wouldn't tell him about the knot that had formed in his middle at the mention of Legal. *Megan.* He'd swear she was clean, but he'd learned to never rule out anyone in an investigation. "Nothing solid, not yet, but I'll work on it. Meanwhile, I've got a problem you can help with."

"Are the boys okay?"

"Oh, they're fine. They love the center and they seem fine with the name change to Diaz. But Mrs. Garner says she has to have an emergency contact in case something happens to the boys and I can't be reached."

Zane frowned. "What about Carmella? She's available."

"She's not really. She's visiting with her sister while we're down here, doing it around her work with the boys."

"What about *your* sister?"

"Aubrey is off playing detective."

"Isn't she an archeologist?"

Rafe shrugged. "The same thing. Dust, bones, excavations, off in the wilds of South America. She's not available. And my mother's in Boston with her sister's family for the month."

"I'll think on it," he said. "Meanwhile, you're here, and if anything happens, which I doubt it will, you're close. If she asks again, tell her you're getting the information.''

"Okay," Rafe said. "I'll check into the staff in Legal."

"Speaking of Legal, that woman you found in Mr. Lawrence's office, the one who you thought was trying to crash the ball?"

He hadn't expected Megan to come up in this conversation. "What about her?"

''Megan Gallagher, right? Tall, blond, smart, pretty?''

"That about sums her up," he said.

"Lindsey called her at the loft about the cat, Joey? Seems that she thought the name sounded familiar, and after she got off the phone, she remembered. Megan Gallagher is the kid sister of Quint Gallagher, our consultant, so you don't need to do any checking on her. She's trustworthy.''

He'd already done his checking, telling himself he was doing it for security reasons, to put any questions about her to rest. He'd found out she was an attorney from San Francisco, that she was here for a month for evaluation, and that she was engaged to Ryan Baron, the son of one of the biggest importer-exporters in the country. Money and more money. But no one had told Rafe about her connection to Quint Gallagher. ''Thanks for the information.''

"Sure," Zane said. "Now, I have to get upstairs. They're waiting for me. Just let me know what you dig up.''

"Of course," he promised.

He let Zane leave first, waiting a few minutes before

he followed. He finally went back toward the lobby, but only as far as the stairs. He was headed upstairs, to have a talk with Wayne Lawrence.

MEGAN STOOD IN THE CENTER of the day care facility and felt as if she'd been abandoned on an island that had been taken over by little people. Children were everywhere, in groups and alone, playing, singing, watching TV, painting and crying—in no particular order. One boy, a beautiful child, had his face puckered up in misery, and was screaming at the top of his lungs. A teenage girl dressed all in black was trying futilely to calm him down.

"Walker, it's okay. Mommy's at the doctor's and you are here to have a good time," the girl said as she tried to interest him in a train that had been set up around a strange-looking play tree in the middle of the room. He let out another scream and hit the train, sending it off its tracks.

Megan had turned away from the piercing confusion, ready to leave and come back later, when she saw an older woman hurrying into the center from the front entrance. She was in her sixties, pleasant looking and dressed in a simple navy dress and white running shoes. She saw Megan, started to smile, then moved faster and called out, "Oh, no!"

Megan didn't know what the woman was yelling about, not until she was blindsided, toppling to her left on the carpet, where she found herself on her back, staring up at a limb of that improbable tree. Pushing herself to a sitting position, she found herself face-to-face with a little boy. His dark brown eyes were wide, his cap of black hair marred by a streak of blue running through it—the same color that stained his beige overalls and white T-shirt.

"Gabriel!" the woman was saying as she reached the child and crouched in front of him, touching his face gently. "Sweetie, you're okay, aren't you?"

Megan pushed herself to her feet while the lady fussed over the little boy, and felt something crack under her shoe. She looked down and saw the earpiece to her phone on the floor. The tiny microphone had snapped right off of the clip. "Damn," she muttered as she stooped to retrieve it and her cell phone.

"Uh-oh, bad word."

She straightened and looked down at the little boy, who was pointing at her accusingly. "That's bad."

She wasn't going to be reprimanded by some kid who was the equal to that beast of a cat at the loft. She couldn't remember the last time she'd fallen, and since she'd been here, she'd taken two tumbles. "No, *this* is bad," she said, holding up the broken earpiece. "Very bad."

Had she really expected to debate with the child, who couldn't be more than five years old? She certainly hadn't expected him to throw himself facedown on the carpet and start to sob with abject misery.

She hadn't meant to make that happen, but didn't know what to do about it once it had. So she crouched to reach for her briefcase, knocked from her hand in the kerfuffle, and that's when she saw her thigh. One tiny handprint stained the linen with the same bright blue that was smeared all over the crying child. Her nerves had been fraying ever since she'd entered this chaos, and this was the last straw. "Look what he did!"

The older lady stood and turned to Megan, frowning at the stain. "I'm so sorry, but I'm sure Gabriel didn't mean to do anything."

"So am I, but my slacks are ruined," Megan muttered, afraid to touch the stain in case that only made it worse. "Absolutely ruined."

She suddenly realized the room was silent, and her words were echoing through it. Mary frowned, and the boy even stopped crying for a moment to stare up at her, his eyes damp with tears. "I'm so sorry," the lady repeated.

Megan made another grab for her briefcase, then straightened. She didn't know what else to say that wouldn't hang her further with the group that was staring at her.

"Gabriel's new here and he's excited. I'm sure he's very sorry for what he did, too." She looked back at the boy. "Aren't you, Gabe?"

He looked at Mary, back to Megan, then started to cry again, huge, silent tears rolling down his cheeks. If she hadn't been the one he'd hit, she would have been furious at anyone who made him cry like that. Just when she was on the verge of trying to make him stop crying, he fell dramatically to the floor once again and started to sob as if his heart would break.

Another little boy ran over, and Megan blinked when she saw him. He was the spitting image of the first boy, but without the blue accents. Identical twins. He was just as dramatic, falling across his brother's back as if shielding him from some unimaginable horror. He whispered something to his brother, then twisted to look up at Megan. Absolutely identical, down to and including those huge dark eyes shooting daggers at her.

The woman patted the second boy on the back, calling him Greg, then a teenage girl hurried over and dropped down by the boys. She gathered them both into her lap, hugging them to her, then she gave Megan a dirty look as she murmured, "It's okay, buddies."

Greg squirmed in the girl's hold and frowned up at Megan again. "You're not nice, lady," he said in a clear, childish voice. The pronouncement carried the same weight as if an adult had called her a jerk. It stung, and only made her more confused, intensifying the feeling she had of being totally out of place.

The woman was at her side now. "Come with me, and we'll take care of your pants," she said.

Megan stared at the children holding on to the teenager, who was rocking them slowly. Gabe was still crying, but Greg just glared. She'd been knocked to the floor. Her earpiece was broken. Her slacks were probably ruined. But for some reason, she was coming out of this disaster as the bad guy, and the fact was she felt like that. *Stupid,* she thought, and turned to follow the woman beyond the tree, down a short hallway, then into an office on the right.

Ever since spotting Rafe that morning, Megan had felt edgy, and now two children had made her nerves raw. She went into the office with the woman who thankfully closed the door on the noise in the other room. Megan looked around the small space, at boxes and files piled against the walls, with a playpen wedged in between. Bookshelves filled the higher walls, and a desk, positioned to face the door, was loaded with paperwork.

Mary motioned to what looked like a pink lawn chair that faced the desk. "Sit and let's take a look at the damage."

Megan put her briefcase on the floor by the pink chair, then sat in it. She still had the remnants of her earpiece in her other hand. "I'm sorry for being so—"

"No, no, forget it," the woman said, then looked up at her with a soft smile. "I'm Mary Garner, by the way. And you must be from Legal?"

"Yes, Megan Gallagher," she said.

"Nice to meet you." Mary looked down at the stain. "I would have preferred a more pleasant greeting, but with kids, you don't have much control over what happens."

Megan knew she needed to apologize, even if it was only for the way she'd spoken out there. "I didn't mean to be so abrupt with the boy."

"And he didn't mean anything by it," Mary murmured, then straightened. "He did a bang-up job of ruining your slacks, though." She started for the door. "I think that's just chalk," she said over her shoulder. "It should come off." Mary left, closing the door behind, and Megan thought she said, "Let me get a brush and I'll give it a try," but she couldn't be sure.

She sank back in the chair, staring at the stain. If she returned to the loft to change, she could be back at work in an hour. Or maybe she should just find a store nearby and buy a new pair of slacks. She couldn't work in these. The door clicked open and Mary was back with a brush in one hand and a white terry cloth rag in the other.

She left the door open, letting the chaotic noise into the small room, and it played across Megan's frayed nerves.

"Now," she said. "We'll fix this up right away."

Megan stood quickly, making sure Mary didn't get within touching range. "No, please, I'll take care of it."

The woman hesitated, brush at the ready. "I'm sure we can get—"

"No, no," Megan said quickly. "I'll take them to the dry cleaners. I don't want to take any chances of permanently ruining them."

Mary held the brush up, but didn't come any closer. "You don't have children, do you?"

That question came out of the blue. "No." Was it that obvious?

"You're an only child?"

"No, I have a brother…an older brother."

Mary nodded as if that explained everything. "Oh, I see."

Megan had no idea just what she thought she saw, because she kept speaking as she went around the desk to sit in the chair and drop the brush and rag by the phone. "Since you're here, maybe we can get a bit of business done before you go to the dry cleaners. If that's okay with you?"

Megan would have gladly sat down and answered any questions Mary had about the legal proceedings, but she never got the chance. Before she could, Greg, the second twin, came barreling into the room, saw her and ran at her full tilt.

She put out her hands to ward him off, her earpiece falling to the floor once more. "Oh, no, you don't!"

The little tornado was stopped in his tracks when someone came in behind him and snatched him up off the floor. It was Rafe! He'd come out of nowhere to rescue her from the kid he was holding in one arm, while the little boy squirmed to get free and wreak more havoc.

Megan met Rafe's gaze, shocked that he seemed on the verge of smiling. "Don't let him go," she said quickly.

"I won't," he promised. "Now, tell me what's going on." He paid no attention whatsoever to the little boy, who had twisted around in his hold and was pressing both hands against his chest to try and escape.

"That…child's brother," she said, bending over to pick up the ruined device again. "He knocked me over, broke my earpiece and smeared blue stuff on my slacks."

She met Rafe's gaze again, and he seemed sober now. "Should I lock him up in jail?" he asked, and his words not only stopped her, but the boy became ominously still, staring up at him.

"What?" she gasped.

He smiled then, an easy, teasing smile that showed a single dimple at the corner of his mouth. "Or I could chain him to a chair for the day, just give him bread and water?"

"Nuh-uh!" the boy said with a quick shake of his head.

"Just kidding, buddy boy," Rafe said to the child, then whispered in his ear. It reminded Megan of the way Greg had whispered in Gabe's ear before giving her that dirty look and telling her she was bad. The boy turned to Megan and that look came again, what her father used to call the "stink eye." It fit. Rafe moved to let him down and Megan braced herself in case he came at her again, but he simply ran out of the room.

Rafe was still there, a teasing glint in his dark eyes that all but made her squirm. "This isn't funny," she said. "And you scared him. You didn't have to do that."

"I thought you wanted revenge."

"Oh, for Pete's sake, that's ridiculous. His brother started it." She opened her hand and showed him the fractured earpiece. "It's ruined," she said.

He glanced at it, then back to her. "He hit you that hard that it broke in two?"

"No, I stepped on it, but…" She bit her lip. "Then he got this all over my clothes." She motioned to the blue stain. "He knocked me over completely."

Rafe came closer, breaching the safe distance between them. "Are you injured?" he finally asked.

She couldn't tell if he was serious or not. "No."

"Any bruises, cuts, scrapes?"

"No, but—"

Rafe abruptly reached for the brush. Moving as fast as the boy had, he hunkered down in front of her and started brushing at the blue on her slacks.

''No, don't!'' she gasped, but he'd didn't stop, and she found herself standing there, frozen, staring down at the top of his guard cap, relishing the sensation as he methodically brushed at her thigh.

Chapter Six

Megan felt fire in her face and closed her eyes tightly while Rafe Diaz brushed at her thigh. When she opened them again, Mary was standing behind him, watching the two of them. She gazed at Rafe intently, then looked up at Megan, and out of the blue gave her a wink.

A wink? Megan looked back at Rafe, at the top of his guard cap, but all she was really aware of was his touch on her leg, an oddly intimate act.

"Good, good, good," Mary murmured when Rafe finally stood.

He faced Megan with just inches separating them. "Gone," he said. "Out, out, damned spot." She must have looked vacant or something, because he said, "Shakespeare."

"I know Shakespeare," she murmured, and looked down at her slacks. She'd definitely lost her dignity, but she'd also lost the spot. The blue was gone. She couldn't believe it, and bent over to take a closer look. Rafe leaned forward at the same time, and her head hit his and she saw stars. *People really see stars,* she thought, as she moved back with a gasp and stumbled against the chair.

Rafe caught her by her shoulders to keep her on her feet. "Oh, my!" she gasped, touching her forehead gingerly with her fingertips as she closed her eyes tightly.

"I'm sorry," he said softly, and she felt the heat of his breath brush her face. She trembled. "Are you okay?"

She opened her eyes, and he was so close his features were blurry. Too close. Much too close. "Yes, I'm okay," she managed to answer, and sank back into the chair behind her.

The instant she sat down, she knew it was a mistake. All it did was make him seem overwhelming as he stood above her. He frowned and bent down, grabbing his hat from the floor, then crouched in front of her, hat in hand. "You're going to have a nasty knot there, maybe a bruise," he said, gesturing to her forehead.

"Great," she muttered. "What else can happen today?"

That made him smile, and she saw the dimple come back, enticingly close to lips that held a soft upward curve. "Don't even ask," he murmured. "Just be careful."

She'd forgotten about Mary until she realized that the older woman was back behind the desk, watching their little show. "As long as those two miniature tornadoes are kept corralled, I think I'll be safe," Megan declared.

"I offered to lock them up," Rafe said easily as he stood, towering over her once again.

She looked up at him, into those dark eyes. "I think taking sugar away from them might be a more reasonable solution. Someone should talk to their mother about their diets."

There was a flash of something in those eyes, something she almost thought was pain. Then she realized it might be anger. There had been a lot of anger at their last encounter. "So, you're an expert on kids, are you?"

"Not even close, but anyone can see that those two little boys need—"

Mary moved closer then, coming around to literally stand between them. "Oh, dear," she murmured with narrowed eyes on Megan's forehead. "I think you need ice." She turned to Rafe. "Could you get some ice for Megan, please?"

Megan knew he didn't want to do anything for her at that moment, but he turned and strode out of the room without a word. The door closed this time with a decidedly hard click. She glanced at the shut door, thankful he was gone, and not feeling any hope that he'd bring back ice.

She gently touched her forehead again and felt the tenderness of swelling. "Ouch," she said, pulling back from the contact. "Is it bruised?"

The woman studied her, then shook her head. "Not yet, but it will be."

"Well, he's got a hard head."

Mary smiled a bit at that. "Most men do."

"I bump heads like that, and then those two kids…" She exhaled. "They're dangerous."

Mary cut her off in midsentence. "Megan, they're his."

She frowned, not understanding. "Excuse me?"

"The twins? Gabe and Greg?"

"Believe me, I haven't forgotten who they are."

"They are his boys. They're Mr. Diaz's sons."

Megan wasn't up to this, not after what she'd said to him about the boys. "Oh, shoot," she muttered. "I didn't know that."

"Of course you didn't," Mary said matter-of-factly. "And you were a bit…stressed."

She rested her head on the back support of the chair and stared up at the acoustical ceiling. Stressed? What a simple word for what Rafe did to her when she was around him. She remembered her idea about him having breakfast with a lot of little Rafes. Now she'd met two of them. And the wife and mother would be right there, too. "Does he have six more at home?" she asked.

"Just the two, I think," Mary said.

Megan stared at the pattern on the acoustic tiles. "They're enough," she muttered.

"I'm sure he thinks so sometimes," the woman said. "How about you—two kids too many?"

She sat up and watched Mary going around to sit behind the desk again. "Excuse me?"

"You know when you're young and you decide, 'I want two boys and two girls,' and you plan your future?"

She was taken aback by that statement. She'd never planned for children, only for school and her career.

"No, I never did," she admitted. "I bet you had a houseful of kids, didn't you?"

Surprisingly, there was no smile now, just a certain sadness in the woman's expression. "I wanted them, but I didn't get them. Now I have a center full of kids." That brought the smile back. "A whole bunch of cute kids."

Now that things were more settled, Megan realized the children probably *were* cute. The twins certainly could be, with huge brown eyes like their father's, midnight-black hair in Buster Brown cuts, and... It was then she realized they both had their father's dimple—one dimple. "As long as I don't have to be around kids much, they're cute, I guess."

Mary laughed softly. "I assume that's an engagement ring?" she asked, glancing at the diamond. "You'll be getting married and having children of your own."

That was a statement, not a question, and Megan wouldn't tell the woman that she and Ryan had never talked about children. She'd assumed they wouldn't be a priority, and maybe would never happen. "Perhaps later on, somewhere down the road, when Ryan and I are settled and things are in order," she murmured. Megan wanted to change the subject. "Why do you suppose the twins went after me?"

Mary laughed ruefully at that. "Oh, honey, they weren't after you, at least not the first time. Gabe was heading for me, and you just got in the way. And Greg, well, he's very, very protective of his brother."

"I'm not some monster," she murmured, though she was sure most people in the center thought she was. "I'm just not good with children," she admitted. "Especially those two little live wires. They are such a handful. I bet they pillage and plunder everywhere they go, and they…"

Her voice trailed off as she realized that Mary was looking past her at someone who had just opened the door and come into the room. Megan's heart sank. She didn't have to look to know that Rafe was back. She'd thought he'd left for good, but here he was, stepping in front of her and holding out a plastic bag of ice. She took it quickly, and chanced a look up at him.

He'd heard her. She knew it by the way his eyes were narrowed and his mouth set. She cleared her throat, and once again apologized to this man. "I'm sorry. I didn't know they were yours, and I didn't mean anything, but they just…they took me by surprise, and I thought my slacks were ruined." She shrugged, implying she was way out of her depth being around the twins. "I'm not used to kids like that," she said in a rush, and knew she'd said the wrong thing once again. One look at his expression made that crystal clear.

There was a nerve-racking silence before he crouched down in front of her, took the bag of ice from her hand and pressed it to her forehead none too gently. She gasped from the sudden rush of cold on the tender spot, and reached up, her hand covering his on the ice bag before he jerked back so quickly that she lost her grip and the bag fell into her lap.

He stared at her hard, then said, "Do it yourself. It might help the swelling." As he stood, he added, "But I don't think it's going to help your attitude at all."

"What the—?"

"Miss Gallagher, you really need to stop judging people, big or small, when you don't know them at all."

Before she could think of something to say, anything, he left, leaving the door open as he disappeared out into the hallway. Megan looked down at the ice bag in her lap and she clenched her hands, the broken earpiece almost cutting into her palm. "Damn it," she muttered.

"Fathers are quite protective, you know," Mary said from behind the desk.

Megan knew that. Or she should have. Her father had been so protective when she was growing up. "He sure is."

"Well, everyone needs someone in this life that they know would go the limit for them, and children really need that more than anyone. Of course, you would probably do that for your Ryan. And I had my dear husband, who would have slain dragons for me."

Megan didn't see Ryan in the roll of dragon slayer, but she wondered how far he'd go for her. Would he rush into a loft when he didn't know if he'd be facing an armed intruder or a fat orange cat? Was Ryan a knight in shining armor? Or was Rafe? She stopped right there when a certain degree of jealousy came out of nowhere as she thought about Rafe protecting his wife. Megan pushed that aside, saying flippantly, "You're a brave lady working here. I'll stay in Legal."

"Speaking of Legal," Mary said. "I'm glad Mr. Lawrence sent you down."

She was more than willing to concentrate on other things. "He told me that you had questions about the day care center incorporation, and asked me to come down to talk it over with you."

"And you ran into a tornado," she said with a slight smile.

"Two of them," Megan murmured, then reached for her briefcase. "I'm here, so ask your questions."

"It's quite confusing, the fund-raising for the charity ball and the attempt to break the day care center's legal ties with LynTech. I admit to not really having the understanding of the process that I should."

The door behind Megan opened, and she turned quickly, a bit giddy with relief that Rafe wasn't there. An older man with snow-white hair, looking very dapper in a well-cut navy suit, was walking into the office. She'd only seen him twice before, once when he'd come to the San Francisco offices and once at the ball, both times from a distance. This was Robert Lewis, the founder of LynTech.

When he saw Megan, he smiled and walked closer with his hand extended. "Hello there. Miss Gallagher, isn't it?"

She had no idea how he knew her name, but she stood, tossed the broken earpiece onto the desk and, clutching the ice bag in her left hand, shook hands with him. "Hello, Mr. Lewis."

"It's good to have you on board," he said, then frowned slightly at her forehead. "My, that looks like a nasty bump. I do hope you're okay."

"It's okay, just a little mishap."

"Good, good," he said as he let her hand go and

glanced past her at Mary. "Mary, I'm sorry to interrupt, but I needed to speak with you right away."

The woman hesitated, and Megan thought she saw a slight flush on her cheeks. "Can't it wait?" she asked.

Mr. Lewis shook his head. "Actually, no, it can't. I only have ten minutes before I need to get to a meeting that might take the rest of the day. This is my only opportunity to get down here." He glanced at Megan. "Would you be so kind as to give us a few minutes?"

Megan looked at Mary. "Go ahead," the woman said, but didn't look happy with the change in plans.

"Okay. I'll be back in fifteen minutes, if that's okay."

"Perfect," Mr. Lewis said, but he wasn't looking at her, he was looking right at Mary.

Megan grabbed her briefcase and the bag of ice, then left quickly. As she turned to pull the door shut behind her, she saw the two people in the room. Mr. Lewis was going around the desk to where Mary was standing, shaking her head and ignoring the hand he held stretched toward her. "If this is about Ray, I don't want to—" The door clicked shut and Mary's words were cut off.

So Ellen had been right about Mr. Lewis and Mary Garner, Megan realized. Stranger things had happened, she thought as she walked out into the main room.

The chaos from moments ago had subsided and the children were gathered in two quiet groups. Older kids she'd seen before were gone, and only tiny children remained, ranging from infants, who were sleeping, to three- or four-year-olds. One group was focused on a

TV cartoon, and the other group was sitting in a circle with the teenage girl she'd seen before, being read to out of a huge book with a blue train engine on the cover.

Megan spotted the twins in the second group, both of them listening with rapt attention to the story while they leaned against each other, connected in some nonphysical way that even she could sense. *A twin thing,* she mused, followed by the thought that, now that they were quiet and still, they looked shockingly angelic. That almost made her laugh. She knew it wasn't the case.

She crossed the room, going past their group, and Gabe, the attacker, glanced up at her as if he sensed her presence. She found herself smiling hesitantly at him, and was stunned when the child smiled shyly back, the dimple deepening. In that instant, he was the spitting image of his father.

She had no idea why that expression made her feel slightly breathless as she kept going toward the exit to make her escape. Escape? That's what it felt like, as if she was getting out through the double entry doors to the center to be able to breathe again and think clearly.

RAFE SAW MEGAN FROM the corner of his eye as she left the center. She was almost out of his peripheral vision, but he knew it was her. Then he glanced away from Brad, another security guard, and looked right at her as she stepped into the elevators. She still had the bag of ice in one hand and her briefcase in the other. As angry as he'd felt at her opinions about the boys, he still had a sneaking suspicion that she was just plain out of her depth with children.

"Hey, she's off-limits," Brad said, getting Rafe's attention.

He looked back at the other guard. "What are you talking about?"

"Miss Ice Princess? The blonde? She's the one from the ball, isn't she? The one you escorted up to Mr. Lawrence?"

"Yes, she is."

"Too bad. She's up there with the big boys, the ones who have the money and the flash."

Rafe wouldn't tell Brad he was right about that, but he didn't like the whole tone of this conversation. "She's an attorney in Legal."

"Yeah, I know. I've seen her around this week, but she looks right through me." He frowned in distaste. "And she'll do the same to you. You can bet on it."

Rafe had been trying to gather a list of people who were in the building at odd hours, when the company records might be accessed a bit more easily. And since Brad worked those hours, Rafe was thinking he might have some ideas about that. But the man was annoying, to say the least. "She works here, just like we do."

Brad laughed at that, quieting a bit when a couple of businessmen gave him a sharp look as they left the building. "Yeah, yeah," he said in a half whisper. "Sure she does. And if you asked her out, she'd accept because we all work in the same building?"

Megan was a snob. She acted superior and probably wouldn't give anyone she thought was beneath her the time of day. But Rafe wouldn't concede that fact to Brad. "Sure, why not?"

"You think you can melt the ice princess?"

Rafe swallowed his distaste, but kept up the banter. "If she weren't engaged, why not?" he repeated.

"Engaged or not, if you can do it, you're on," Brad said, and extended his hand to him. "Ten bucks?"

"Ten dollars?"

"Okay, make it twenty." His hand was still shoved toward Rafe. "Or maybe you don't have it in you? Maybe I should make it more and let you watch?"

At any other time, Rafe would have punched the man's lights out, but all he did was stare at him while he thought of this lug making passes at Megan. That did it. He put his hand in Brad's. "Fifty."

The man hesitated, his face infused with a touch of color. Rafe didn't miss the way he swallowed before agreeing. "You're on. How long?"

Megan would be out of here soon. "Why not. Two weeks. Deal?"

"Okay," Brad said, then looked at the clipboard in his hand. "I really came down here to tell you you've got to do two graveyards this week."

"I can't do graveyard."

"Tell that to the boss. We all have to do it on rotation." He made a dismissive motion to the cavernous entryway where they stood. "Glitz and glitter has to be protected, you know. Keep the money where it is."

"It doesn't matter what we're protecting, does it, as long as we get paid?"

"Yeah, that's the thing. Getting paid." Brad lowered his voice. "The big suits are all upstairs. Seems there's been something going on, but even if we wear the guns, we're not being included.''

''They'll let us know what we need to know,'' Rafe said, and made a mental note to check on the person who did the screenings for Dagget Security here in Houston.

''You'd better get up to Security,'' Brad said, tapping his wristwatch. ''They watch your ticket and you don't want to get written up for inactivity.''

He was right about that policy, and Rafe didn't want to draw any unnecessary attention to himself. ''Sure,'' he said, and headed back into the building. He veered off at the day care center, went inside and stayed just out of sight of the main room to check on the boys. They were quietly listening as a teenager read to them. The whole explosion with Megan seemed to have blown over. He backed out and headed for the elevators.

The rest of the day was gone before he knew it, and he hadn't even stopped for lunch. He'd thought he'd go to the center and eat with the boys, as Mary had suggested, but he never made it. Instead, when he'd gone up to Security, his supervisor had assigned him to the below ground parking garage and that structure's exit, asking him to keep a log on whomever came and went, and the times. He didn't have a clue why they'd want that. It was nothing he'd suggested to Zane, and not company policy, but it couldn't hurt.

As soon as he went into the garage, he saw Megan's car, and for the rest of the day he was very aware of it being there, and never moving. At five o'clock Rafe closed out his shift, signed off at the gate, then headed across the garage to go up and clock out. He glanced to his right and saw that Megan's car was still there, two stalls over from his SUV. She hadn't been down all day.

He pulled the door open to go into the building and came face-to-face with her as if his thoughts had conjured her up. Megan had slightly mussed hair, no lipstick and a new earpiece attached to the phone peeking out of her breast pocket. She had an armful of files, along with her briefcase, and her blue eyes were totally unreadable.

She slipped past him without a word, and he remembered what Brad had said earlier, about her looking through him. Rafe should have gone in the opposite direction and closed the door on her, but he didn't. He found himself turning toward her as she headed for her car. "Miss Gallagher?" he called.

MEGAN HADN'T KNOWN what to say when she saw Rafe in front of her, so she had walked right past without a word. She was halfway to her car when he called her name. She stopped, considered ignoring him, but didn't.

She turned and spotted him over by the security door. "Yes?"

He hesitated, then took his hat off, holding it in both hands by the band. Was he going to apologize for what his kids had done to her? Or was he going to warn her again about the dangers of living at the loft? Neither of those things happened. Instead, he asked, "How's the cat?"

She'd totally forgotten about the cat. He came, he

went, he ate. And since Mrs. Holden had asked her to let him be there, she'd tried to ignore him. "He's probably taking over the world as we speak."

Rafe laughed softly, a warm rich sound that was all too fleeting. "He's tough," he said.

"Yes, he is."

He hesitated again, then said, "Your slacks, are they okay?" He glanced down at her legs.

"Sure. Fine."

"Your head…" He motioned to the spot they'd bumped each other. "It's okay?"

"Yes, it didn't even bruise very much."

"Good. Good."

They faced each other awkwardly, and she couldn't think of another thing to say. So she shrugged slightly, gripping the files in her arms. "I need to get these things in the car. Homework."

"Sure. Have a good evening," he said, slipping his hat back on. With a nod, he opened the door and disappeared inside the building.

Megan watched the door click shut, wondering what that was all about, then she got to her car. She put her things in the back, then sank into the seat. As she touched the steering wheel, she noticed that her hands weren't quite steady. She reached for the replacement earpiece she'd found on her lunch hour, clicked the On button by the microphone and put in a call to Ryan at work, got no answer, then tried his home. "Ryan. Home." Once the number was connected, it rang twice, then she got his voice mail. Obviously he wasn't there either. "Ryan, it's Megan. I just wanted to…" She exhaled, not sure what she wanted to do.

''I just wanted to say hi and see how you're doing. I'll call later.'' She clicked off and started the car.

She exhaled, then put the car in gear and would have driven to the exit if another car hadn't pulled out of a stall and cut right in front of her. She braked hard, and the other car kept going to the security gate. She looked to her right, and saw that everything she'd had on the seat had slid off on to the front passenger floor mat. She stretched to pick it all up, and when she lifted a brown envelope, realized she hadn't given certain vital paperwork to Mary. She'd promised her some rough drafts by five, and she'd worked on them, but had totally forgotten to stop by and give them to her.

Megan turned off the car, grabbed the envelope and her car keys, then climbed out and hit the alarm as she headed for the door into the building. Where there had been people everywhere just minutes ago, now the hall was totally empty, and soft background music that was piped through all the public areas during the day had been shut off. The hush made the sound of her shoes hitting the hard floors ring in the emptiness.

She walked quickly toward the bright doors of the center, and when she got within ten feet of the entrance to Just For Kids, the door nearest her opened. She hesitated, for a moment worried that Rafe would be coming out. But it wasn't Rafe who emerged, it was his tiny double. One of the twins. Gabe? Greg? She wasn't sure, but his overalls were clean, so maybe it was Greg, the one who had kept giving her ''the look'' earlier.

The door swung shut behind him, then he pushed his little hands in his pockets and headed toward the front entrance of the building. *A kid on a mission,* she thought as she went closer, watching him walk determinedly toward the exit. She expected Rafe to come into the lobby, or Mary, or even one of the teenagers who worked at the center, but no one showed up. And the child was almost at the exit doors, the only barriers between him and the busy street outside.

She reached for the center door to go in and get someone, but stopped when she saw the child reach out, pressing both tiny hands against the glass barrier. She hesitated, then did the only thing she could do. She went after him, calling out, ''Hey there, little boy, hey!''

Chapter Seven

The child didn't turn, and he didn't stop trying to push the doors open.

"Hey, little guy!" she called as she caught up to him.

He had both hands on the glass, pushing as hard as he could against them. She could see his face in the reflection, and his expression was one of fierce determination, his mouth set, his eyes scrunched tightly with the effort.

"Hey, buddy boy," she said, using the nickname Rafe had used earlier.

The boy didn't stop trying to make his escape, but he did turn his head in her direction and look up at her. When he saw who was there, he turned back to the door and pushed even harder.

"You can't go out there alone," she said. The boy ignored her.

She remembered her brother, Quint, when he was talking to his daughter, Taylor. He always crouched down in front of her. "Don't tower over them," he'd told her. "Get to eye level." So she did. She crouched by the boy. "What are you doing?"

"Going," he muttered as he kept up the fruitless pushing.

"Where are you going?"

"To find Mama," he said, then closed his eyes again, lowered his head and pushed harder. The door wasn't going to open for him, and he must have realized it, because he stopped. His exhaled sigh shuddered through his little body, and she had the startling urge to hug him to her. She clenched her jaw and did no such thing.

He really wanted to get to his mother. "Honey, you can't go out there alone," she said, thinking she was making perfect sense.

He looked at her then, and his chocolate-brown eyes were overly bright, as if he'd been crying or was about to. Then she saw the dimple, so much like his father's. And for some reason she realized that Gabe had a dimple on his right cheek, like his dad did, but Greg had a dimple on his left. This was Gabe, the dramatic one. The crier. She hoped against hope that he wasn't gearing up for another crying session.

He pointed to the door. "Open it."

"Why don't we go and get your daddy?" she suggested.

"No," he said quickly, his bottom lip in a full pout now.

"Well, you can't go out there," she said in as even a voice as she could muster. "There's big cars out there, and they go fast and they can hurt you."

He frowned, looked out the glass door, then back

at her. His bottom lip wasn't at all steady now. "Want out," he mumbled.

"Well, we all do, but sometimes it's not a good idea," she said. *Always give them a way out,* Quint had told her. "Tell you what, why don't you come with me, and we'll find someone who can let you out so you can go see your mother?"

He frowned at her, and Megan held her breath, hoping he'd buy into that rationale. But he said, "You mad?"

"Me, mad?" she asked.

He nodded once. "Uh-huh."

"No, no, I'm not mad." She tried to smile, and found it was easy to do so. "I'm not mad at all." She pushed her luck just a bit by holding out her hand to him. "Come on. Why don't we go looking for someone to help you out?"

He jerked his hands behind his back and shook his head. "No, you...you're strange," he said with total seriousness.

Strange? Then she understood. "I'm a stranger, is that what you mean?"

He nodded emphatically.

"And your daddy told you never to go with strangers, didn't he?"

He nodded again.

"Good, that's a good boy. You shouldn't. You're really smart. You should never go with a stranger, not anywhere. But I'm not a stranger. You met me before," she said, and wished she hadn't reminded him when his eyes got wider. "Okay, that was a mistake, an accident, but it's okay, and I know your dad and

Mary, Mrs. Garner. And I work here.'' She knew enough not to push too hard. ''Why don't you come with me, but you don't have to take my hand, okay?''

She saw him falter, then he nodded. ''Okay.''

She wanted to pump her arm and shout, ''Yes!'' but merely stood and said, ''Okay then, let's go.''

She started back toward the center, moving slowly so that he could keep up. With the envelope and her keys in her left hand, she kept her right hand ready to grab at him if he took off. But he didn't. In fact, as they neared the doors, he quite unexpectedly took hold of her hand, his tiny fingers curling around two of her fingers. And she was totally unprepared for the lurch in her heart. ''Good,'' she said softly, startled that he felt so tiny and that she felt so overwhelmingly protective at that moment.

She'd never felt that way in her life—that sense of being the only person available to keep another human being safe. She was going off the deep end, she thought. It wasn't as though she'd taken a bullet for someone, or stepped into the path of a speeding car to save him. She just had been there and managed to stop this little boy from leaving.

As they got to the center, the far door flew open and Rafe was there yelling, ''Gabe!''

He froze when he saw them, then came toward them and had Gabe in his arms so fast that it was all a blur. He was hugging the boy to him, and the look in his eyes, the expression on his face of such heart-wrenching relief, hit her hard. He was scared to death, and all she wanted to do was tell him it was okay, that everything was fine. Another first for her, and another disturbing reaction.

"He's okay," she managed to say, although she wasn't sure Rafe was listening to her.

"What were you doing?" he was asking the boy, holding Gabe back so he could look in his face. "Where were you going?"

"Going to Mama." The voice was tiny and quavering, but it could have been as strong as a trumpet's peal for the reaction it had on Rafe. The pain produced in his eyes because of those three simple words tore at Megan.

Rafe hugged Gabe to him. "Oh, buddy boy, you can't. And you can't do this again, either. You scared me a lot." He exhaled. "You can't leave me. Not now," he finished in a rough whisper.

The little boy buried his face in his father's shoulder and patted his back slowly. "Promise, never, never, do that again," he said in a low voice.

Then the door opened once more, and Mary was there with Greg in tow. He ran at his dad, attacking him at knee level and hanging on to him tightly. "Gabe, Gabe," he said, and his brother twisted in his father's arms. The next instant, Gabe wiggled down onto the ground, facing his twin, then both of them turned at the same time to look at Megan. Gabe's eyes were soft and vulnerable, wrenching her heart, but Greg glared at her. "You're bad," he muttered. "Real bad."

Gabe grabbed his brother, whispered something to him, and whatever he said changed everything. Greg looked back at her, cocked his head to one side to study her intently, and she thought he was going to say something. But he didn't. Instead, he grabbed his brother's hand and spoke to Rafe. "We got to clean blocks."

Mary nodded. "I'll take them, Mr. Diaz. I can't tell you how sorry I am that we got distracted. It's never happened before and—"

Rafe cut her off. "Please, it wasn't your fault."

Megan realized she was standing there holding the envelope for Mary. "Mrs. Garner, here," she said, and held it out. "The papers you needed?"

"Oh, yes, thank you, dear," the woman said, taking the envelope. "I'm coming, you two," she called out as she went back into the center after the boys.

Then it was just Rafe and Megan, and she could see the way he was collecting himself—the shuddering sigh, then the deep breath, and finally, those dark eyes on her. "Okay, what happened?"

"I saw him come out and go to the door. He was leaving, and if he'd been any stronger, he would have been out on the street."

He ran a hand roughly over his face. "Thank you for stopping him."

She shrugged, uncomfortable with him seeing her as a rescuer. "Well, he couldn't open the door."

"Just the same…" He shook his head sharply as if to clear it. "Thank you."

"Sure. He just wanted to see his mommy," she murmured for something to say, then wished she hadn't said anything.

Words meant to fill in spaces were potent enough

to make Rafe pale slightly and his eyes become flat. ''His mommy,'' he echoed.

''That's what he said. He seemed pretty determined to get home to her.''

He exhaled. ''He can't get home to her,'' Rafe said in a low, rough whisper.

''She's gone?''

He exhaled again, as if he couldn't quite catch his breath. ''She's gone. She passed away. I lost her. We lost her.''

Megan stared at him, his words sinking in. ''She's...?''

''Dead. She's dead,'' he said with more power in his voice. ''I hate the euphemisms for it. People never say, 'She died. She's dead.' They have these phrases that they make up so it doesn't sound so bad.'' He had unconsciously begun to twist his wedding band, and Megan was stunned at how she could feel his pain. It wasn't even sympathy, but a gut knowledge that his grief was almost beyond bearing. He had to have loved her more than life itself. Megan wasn't used to this sort of feeling, or the staggering need to make his pain stop.

''I'm so sorry!'' That was all she could get out right then, and it sounded so ineffective.

''Sure, everyone is,'' he breathed, then must have realized what he was doing with his ring, because he stopped abruptly. He pushed his hands into the pockets of his slacks. ''Sorry to get into this,'' he said. ''It's been two years, but I think that some kid in there must have said something about his mom, maybe that she was coming for him. I don't know. I was talking to

Mrs. Garner when Gabe obviously decided he was leaving to find his mom.''

''Probably,'' Megan said, thinking a child would believe that just going to find someone would work. Maybe young ones couldn't fathom death.

''Thanks again for stopping him.''

''Of course.''

Rafe hesitated, as if he wanted to say more, but he didn't. He just went back into the center and left her standing there.

She stood unmoving for a moment, realizing how shaken she was by the past ten minutes. Life was strange, and people were never what you thought they were.

She headed back to the parking garage. *You really need to stop judging people, big or small, when you don't know them at all.* Rafe's words resonated because that's just what she'd been doing. And once again, she owed him an apology.

FOR THE NEXT WEEK, Megan spent more time at the center than she did at the loft or in her cubicle in Legal on the nineteenth floor. She didn't see Rafe except in passing, but she saw Gabe and Greg every day except for the weekend. Saturday and Sunday she spent at the loft, working and trying to ignore the partying in the next loft.

On Thursday, she stayed upstairs in her cubicle and worked straight through lunch. By five, she'd loaded her car with the paperwork she had to take home, and had made one last trip up to the office to check her messages. But Mr. Lawrence called her, catching her at her desk, and reminded her that Mary Garner needed some numbers by five. The work had to be ready to go the next morning. Megan grabbed the folder and carried it along with her car keys down to the center.

When she walked in, she saw both boys immediately. Only four children were left, and Greg and Gabe were in the middle of finger painting with the others under the guidance of a woman with fiery red hair— Brittany Terrell, married to the CEO, Matt Terrell.

When Gabe spotted her, he smiled and waved a bright red hand. Megan smiled back, and realized that he was a particularly likable child. Since she'd made her "rescue," he seemed to think that they were friends, and she was fine with that as long as the red hands didn't touch her off-white slacks or her beige silk blouse.

Greg, on the other hand, wasn't angry at her anymore, but he kept his distance, warily sizing her up and keeping a close eye on her when she talked to Gabe. She smiled at Greg, but got nothing in return, so she looked for Mary. The older woman wasn't in sight, however.

Brittany got to her feet, said something to the boy beside her, then came across to Megan. "Do you need something?"

She flinched when Greg splattered a bunch of bright yellow paint on the paper in front of him on the floor. Brittany saw what she was looking at and said, "Don't worry. Anthony, my son, is tough. He'll make sure they don't destroy the world while I'm not watching." So that boy, Anthony, was her son? They looked nothing alike, but Megan didn't miss the connection between them. Or the way Brittany smiled when she looked back at him. "The little darlings," she murmured. Then she gazed at Megan. "Now, what can I do for you?"

"I need to leave some paperwork for Mrs. Garner."

"There's a never-ending flow of paperwork in this business," she said. "You'd think with the way computers are taking over the world, the trees would be safe, but no way."

Megan smiled, liking her and the fact that they were almost the same height. There weren't many women who met her eye to eye.

"Can you just leave the papers with me?"

"I guess, but I don't know if Mrs. Garner has questions."

Brittany came a bit closer and lowered her voice. "Well, between you and me, she's busy." She grinned as if she were the cat who ate the canary. "Seems she's in the office talking with my father and another man. They didn't look happy when they went in, and they've been in there awhile."

"Well, I guess I'll just wait."

Brittany touched her arm lightly. "You know what? Why don't you just go on in? I would, but I promised Mary I wouldn't let the kids out of my sight." She hesitated, then said, "If you want to watch the kids, I could go in and let Mary know you're here. I'm dying to find out why Dad's in there."

"Dad?"

"Robert Lewis. He's my father."

Megan had had no idea. "Oh," she murmured weakly.

"So, can you watch them for a bit?"

She hesitated, and finally said, "I'll go on in and let Mary know I'm here."

But she didn't have to do that. There was the sound of voices, then Robert Lewis came out of the back hallway. He glanced at Brittany, and said briskly, "See you at the house," then looked at Anthony—his nine-year-old grandson, Megan realized. "Don't be late," he advised, and then was gone.

Before Megan could say anything, another man came down the hallway, a lean gentleman in his middle sixties, wearing jeans, boots and a simple white shirt that contrasted starkly with his tanned skin. He saw Megan and Brittany, nodded to them and kept going right out of the center.

"Oh, boy," Brittany muttered, but before she could say anything else Mary arrived, looking flustered. When she saw them, she stopped, taking the time to smooth her hair before she came closer. Brittany said, "The Barnes boy will be picked up in a few minutes. His mother got tied up with work. And the twins are heading out by six. Anthony and I are off to Dad's tonight for dinner. Matt has to work late."

They had said Rafe would be there at six to get the boys, so Megan had a while to get out. She hadn't really spoken to him since that day when Gabe had tried to leave, and she was certain Rafe was trying to avoid her. Not that she blamed him, after what she'd said about the boys' mother, his wife.

"Thanks, Brittany," Mary said. "If you could put away the paper, it would be very appreciated."

"Of course." The other woman looked at Megan. "Fun, fun, fun," she said, and headed off to collect the scattered pages on the floor.

"Do you have those copies for me?" Mary asked.

"Oh, yes. Here." She handed her the file. "The contracts are in there, and also the readouts of the funding procedure you agreed on before. Some charts of the expenses, as well."

"A little light reading before bed," she joked as she took the papers.

Welcome to the club, Megan thought. She had tons of reading ahead of her tonight, too. "Just let me know if you have any questions?"

Brittany reappeared. "Anthony and I are leaving now."

"Thanks for the help," Mary said. Brittany said her goodbyes and the two of them left.

Gabe and Greg were in the corner, Megan noticed, cleaned up from the paint and hunkered down over something she couldn't see.

"These are the final readouts?" Mary asked her.

"Yes, I believe so." Then she remembered something. "Oh, darn, I was supposed to pick up an envelope for you at the desk in Legal and I totally forgot. Ellen had it—still has it," she said with a grimace. "She was there when I left, so—"

"No problem." Mary started toward the center entranceway. "I'll go and get it from Ellen. Stay with the kids for a few minutes?" She didn't wait for a response before she was out the door.

"Great," Megan muttered, glancing at the boys, who were still focused on something across the room. She looked around, then shrugged. "A few minutes." She could do a few minutes.

She moved back, saw a small bench by the climbing tree and sank down on it, feeling like Gulliver in the land of the Lilliputians. She looked over at the boys, who both stood and gazed over their shoulders at her at the same time. Once the Barnes boy was picked up, Megan turned her attention back to the twins.

One whispered something to the other, then with their hands behind their backs, they came over to stand in front of her, one behind the other. Greg was the closest.

"What are you two up to?" she asked warily.

"Here," Greg said, and thrust something toward her that he cradled in both hands.

She looked down at the biggest rat she'd ever seen, just inches from her face, and couldn't stop the scream.

RAFE HEARD A SHATTERING scream just as he approached the doors to the center, and without taking time to think, he rushed inside. Gabe and Greg were running around the main room, chasing something. Then he saw her—Megan. She was scrambling to get up off the floor, pushing a small stool to one side to make room, and she was yelling, "Catch it! Catch it!" to the boys as she hugged her arms around herself.

The boys were squealing, rushing behind the tree. When they came out the other side, Rafe finally saw what they were after. A rat. A huge white-and-black rat, outrunning the boys and heading straight for Megan. She saw it at the same time he did, and moved faster than anyone he'd ever seen move in his life. She darted to her right, away from the tree and right toward him.

He held out his hands and managed to partially break the impact when they collided, but he couldn't stop her impetus. Falling backward, Rafe felt a jumble of softness and heat, then was drenched in that subtle fragrance that he realized was unique to Megan. Moments later he found himself on the floor, flat on his back, with Megan above him, her body pressed along the length of his.

Those blue eyes widened, then there was a gasp and she moved back. He pushed himself up onto his elbows and watched her scramble to her feet. Pale slacks that he'd bet had been immaculate moments ago were rumpled and had smudges of green on one hip now. Her silky blouse had come untucked on one side, the top button undone, and one errant strand of hair had escaped from the confines of a low knot.

She looked down at him, shock stamped on her face, then spun around. The boys were going into the opening of the tree, scrambling in one after the other. When they'd disappeared, their squeals of delight still echoed out of the opening. "Get him," Megan called, hurrying over to the tree. She dropped to her knees, looking inside. "Get him!"

Rafe pushed himself to his feet, then followed, tempted to tap her on the bottom to get her attention. But he controlled himself and simply said, "Excuse me?"

''Hurry, hurry, he'll get to the other side!''

''Hello?'' he said, hunkering down by her and finally letting himself touch her back. He felt the silkiness of the blouse and the feel of her heat under that fine material. He drew back quickly, then said louder, ''Megan, hello?''

She scooted back on her heels, then looked up at him. ''It's a rat. Greg tried to give it to me.''

''He what?''

''A rat. A huge rat, and I screamed and fell and it got away, and they're trying to catch it.''

Rafe looked at her, at her huge blue eyes. ''They were tormenting you with a rat?'' he asked, trying very hard not to smile at the way she jumped when one of the boys yelled, ''There, over there!''

She got to her feet, looking around the room. ''Don't just stand there. Do something,'' she said.

''Like what?''

She shook her hands quickly, as if trying to get rid of a creepy feeling. ''I don't know!'' she exclaimed, almost jumping up and down now. ''Just get him.''

She was clearly terrified of the animal—very likely the resident rat called Charlie, part of the day care center's menagerie. ''I've got a gun,'' Rafe said, making a joke.

She looked horrified. ''Oh, no, no,'' she gasped, before realization dawned. ''That's not funny!''

Right then one of the twins scrambled out of the tree and pushed between the two of them. ''We got him,'' he announced, and started to hold the rat up toward Megan.

Rafe picked up the animal gently but deftly. ''I'll

take that thing,'' he said, holding the squirming rat carefully in both hands. "Now, you two tell me what you think you were doing, scaring Megan like that.''

Unexpectedly, she interrupted. "No, that wasn't what happened.'' Both boys looked up at her now. "They were just showing it to me…I think. I hate rats, and I overreacted. It wasn't their fault.''

Both sets of dark eyes were on him now. Rafe hesitated. "Is that true?'' he asked the boys.

Greg spoke up. "Gabe said she'd like Charlie, and he told me to show it to her.''

A gift to Megan? That shocked Rafe as much as her scream had moments ago. Neither boy, but especially Gabe, had taken to many women since their mother's death. And heaven knew Megan wasn't trying to win them over. That thought stopped him. Win them over? No, she wouldn't do that; he was certain of it. Yet in some way she had. "Okay. Just apologize, and next time, warn her, okay?''

They both nodded. Rafe gave the rat to Greg, who turned to Megan, holding the animal against his chest. "Sorry,'' he said.

Gabe stood there, head down, and Rafe touched his hair. "Son, apologize.''

He exhaled, then looked up at Megan. "Sorry,'' he mumbled.

Rafe wasn't sure what to expect of Megan, but it wasn't to see her crouch in front of both boys and actually smile at them. "It's the thought that counts,'' she said. "And as far as rats go, I'm sure he's a lovely one. I just never liked the creatures.''

"Girls don't,'' Greg said.

"This girl doesn't."

"Why don't you two put him away and make sure he's got water?" Rafe said.

Greg turned and darted off with the rat, but Gabe hung back, then dug his hand into his overalls pocket and held something out to Megan. "Here," he said. "It's okay."

It was a cookie with a distinct bite out of one side and something red on the other. Megan looked at the object in his small hand, then smiled at Gabe. "For me?"

"Uh-huh," he said with a nod.

Rafe held his breath, knowing how much it meant to Gabe to have her take it, but not sure she'd do so. "Well, thank you. This is so nice of you." She took the cookie, and Rafe breathed again.

Gabe darted off after his brother, and Rafe looked at Megan, who was staring at the cookie in her hand. "First a rat, now…"

"A half-eaten cookie, and it's chocolate chip, which is one of his absolute favorites." Rafe tried to sound casual, but he was stunned by what had just happened. "You are such a liar," he found himself saying.

"Excuse me?" she asked, her blue eyes widening.

"You said that you weren't good with kids."

She blushed at his words. "I'm not. Believe me."

"You've got a magic touch with the boys. They don't like many people, and for Gabe to give you his cookie…" Rafe shrugged. "All I can say is you're one lucky lady." He moved closer and touched the cookie she still held in her open hand. "And you've got an extra something on it, too.'' He tapped the red area. ''Any idea what that is?''

He leaned in to get a better look at the cookie at the same she did. This time, though, she jerked back just before they hit heads again. The cookie fell to the floor and he stooped to get it, then looked at her. ''Stand back. I think we're pretty lethal when we get too close.''

Words meant to be a joke made her face flame, and Rafe tried to think of something, anything to blot out the images that were there with crystal clarity. Her against him. Him touching her. The kiss. He'd blocked all of it out until this moment, and now the memories came rushing back. They stood there, their eyes locked, and he didn't know what to do, what to say. Because if he did what he wanted right then, he wouldn't be able to stop.

Chapter Eight

Megan hurried past Rafe, calling to Mary, as soon as she saw her return, "Good, you're back. I need to get going."

"Of course, dear," the woman said as Megan went through the door, never looking back at Rafe or the boys. "And thank you for the paperwork!"

Megan crossed over to the elevators, got in and hit the button. Moments later she stepped out in Legal and stopped dead.

This wasn't where she was supposed to be going. She was supposed to be heading to her car. She'd been ready to leave before she went down to the center. Whatever had gone on with Rafe had left her flustered, and she hadn't been thinking clearly. She looked around and noted Ellen was nowhere in sight. Megan went past reception and back to her cubicle.

She sank down on the chair behind her desk, took her earpiece out of her pocket and adjusted it, then said into the microphone, "Ryan. Home." She hadn't been able to reach him for two days, and the last time they talked, he'd been very distracted. Now she really needed to speak to him.

When the call connected, she waited through four rings. Just when she thought she was going to get Ryan's machine again, he answered, and the sound of his voice, so familiar and sane, made her eyes smart.

"Ryan, it's me."

"Megan. Hi, there." He didn't stop at that, but kept speaking quickly. "You caught me at a bad time. I've got a huge meeting with Lennox, the attorney, and I need to get out of here right now."

"Sure," she said, almost tasting her disappointment. "I just wanted to…" What? What did she want?

"Anything important?"

"No, it's not important. Can you call me later?"

"Can't promise, but I'll try," he said. With a quick, "Bye, love," he was gone.

She hit the Disconnect button and sank back in her chair. What had she expected? To hear Ryan's voice and find her balance again? "Stupid," she muttered, and stood.

She headed back out and was surprised to see Ellen back at her desk, pushing things into her purse. She must have heard Megan's steps on the marble floors, because she turned quickly, looking vaguely guilty about something. Ellen exhaled as she pressed a hand to her chest. "Oh, you startled me. I thought everyone was gone for the evening."

"I was gone, but had to come back up."

"Oh, if you were looking for the papers for the center, Mary Garner—"

"I know, I took care of it. I just had to make a call." She passed the desk where the woman was standing. "I'm leaving."

"Have a good evening," Ellen said.

"You, too." Megan got back in the elevator and turned to push the button for the ground level. Ellen was stuffing an envelope into her purse, then she glanced up, gave Megan a forced smile, and the doors of the elevator closed.

Megan closed her eyes tightly as the elevator went downward. When a soft ding signaled the stop and the doors opened, she hesitated, then looked out into an empty hallway. She exited, glanced at the closed doors of the center, and headed back toward the parking garage. She didn't pause until she was at her car, then stopped dead. Her keys. The keys for the car, and the alarm button. She didn't have anything in her hands.

She looked in car windows to make sure she hadn't left the keys in there. But all she saw was her briefcase, her files and the box of letters. Everything but her keys. Then she remembered she'd taken the keys with her to the center. "Damn, damn, damn," she muttered, and slapped the top of the car with the palm of her hand.

Reluctantly, she went back into the building. But when she got to the center, the doors were locked. Mary must be gone, and it was shut up for the night. Megan exhaled. The keys had to be inside, and she had to get in there.

She glanced at her watch and saw it was almost six-thirty. Rafe had to be gone by now. Megan headed to the guard station at the front doors, but it was vacant.

She went to the floor directory, saw that Security was on the second floor, and went back to the elevators. Moments later she was walking down a long hallway toward the security office. Stepping inside, she saw that the space was large, with monitors lining one wall, computers on several desks and a starkly utilitarian feel to the operation. At first she thought it was vacant, then she saw a guard off to the left near a filing cabinet. She cleared her throat and he turned abruptly.

"I'm sorry to bother you, but I need to get into the day care center. I left my car keys in there, and it's locked up."

She thought he was the same guard who had come to the gates at the ball to take Rafe's place. The man frowned at her, then walked across the room. "Locked out, huh?"

"Yes, I didn't realize my keys were in there until it was too late. I hope you can help me?"

"Sure, no problem." He reached for a phone on the nearest desk, punched in several numbers, then spoke into the receiver. "Meet an employee at the day care center, and—" He stopped abruptly, frowned, then said, "It won't take two minutes. Just open up for her." He listened for a moment, then hung up. "You go on down, and someone will be waiting for you. Just show him your ID and he'll open up the center."

Her ID? It was in her briefcase in the car. "Thanks so much," Megan said, and headed back down again, trying to figure out how to prove who she was to the guard. When she stepped out of the elevator, she saw that the door to the center was partially ajar. She pushed it open and entered the room, which was softly lit by security lights around the ceiling.

"Hello?" she called out. "The man upstairs sent me down to get my keys."

As she stepped forward she sensed movement to her right, and turned just as Rafe came out of the shadows. Her heart lurched. He was supposed to have left with his kids, not be emerging out of the shadows, with his cap gone, his tie undone and his uniform shirt unbuttoned at the throat.

"You're not supposed to be here," she said.

"Oh? And you are?" he asked.

"I meant, you were supposed to be off duty."

He shrugged. "Sorry I'm still here. But I'm more than willing to leave if you don't need me."

"I'll just look around for my keys. Go ahead and leave, and I'll close up when I find them," she said, a bit uneasy that the twins might run out at any moment and bring the rat with them. "Where are your boys?"

"Home with their baby-sitter. I pulled some extra time when someone else didn't show up for work and Carmella came to get them. And I can't leave you alone here. I need to lock up, make sure things are secure." He waved a hand in a sweeping motion. "Go ahead, take your best shot. Look for your keys. I'll wait."

That's what she was afraid of. Him waiting right there, watching her. She turned and headed to the tree, toward the stool she'd used. But as she looked for her keys, all she really was aware of was Rafe, watching her. She dropped to her knees on the carpet, pushing a hand into the hole in the tree and groping around. But she didn't feel anything.

"Any luck?" Rafe asked from behind her.

She stood and turned. "No." She brushed her hands together. "Mary must have found them."

"That's possible," he conceded. "I could call her, but I think she mentioned she was going out for the evening." He moved off into the shadows past the tree. "I'll look in her office and see if she put them in there," he called over his shoulder.

He was lost in the dimness until a light flashed, spilling out into the hallway from Mary's office. Megan heard shuffling, then a thumping sound, and she remembered him going into her loft to look for the "intruder." Then, she'd been afraid he'd be hurt, that he'd encounter something dangerous, but now she was afraid for herself.

The light went out and she knew he was coming back. She took a tight breath. There was nothing remotely personal about what they were doing in here, but she felt an intimacy that was totally out of order, and crazy.

She moved back as he came closer. "No keys in there, unless she locked them up somewhere," he said.

"I can probably get replacement keys from the car rental agency, but the loft keys—"

"It may already be closed."

"Then I'll call a taxi." That wouldn't help. Even if she got a cab, and borrowed money from Rafe to pay for it, she couldn't get into the loft without the keys. "Never mind. I can't get into the loft. The ring had all my keys on it."

"Come on," he said. "I need to lock up."

She didn't have much choice in the matter, so she went with him out of the center. He locked the doors then turned to her. "Use your phone to call the car rental company," he said, and took out his own cell phone. "I'll work on the loft."

Before she could ask him what he thought he could do, he was already punching in a number. She found her earpiece, put it on and called the car company. She was aware of Rafe speaking, but didn't follow his conversation while she went through the automated options at the rental center. But it was all for nothing. There was no live person to talk to, just a voice mail where she could leave a phone number for emergency towing. She left her cell phone number, just in case, then hung up.

She turned to Rafe, who was still on the phone. "Okay, you're sure that he'll be able to let her in?" He listened, then said, "Thanks. I'll take it from there." Flipping his phone closed, he pushed it back in his pocket. "Okay, you can get into the loft. One of the tenants has an extra set of keys. Seems they were left so the cat could be fed if he came back and no one was there." Rafe grinned at her, a very unexpected and endearing expression. "That cat came through for you, kid."

"Remind me to give him extra tuna," she murmured, looking away from the smile and the dark eyes touched by it. "I'll call a taxi and get—"

"You don't have to."

She hesitated. "Why not?"

He glanced at his watch, then said, "I'm off in two

minutes. I've got my car in the garage and I'm going that way.''

She knew it wasn't a good idea to have him drive her home, but she couldn't figure out why. "Oh, no, you've got things to do, I'm sure, and that's an inconvenience.''

"No, and no.''

"Excuse me?''

"No, I don't have things to do, except go home, and no, it's not an inconvenience.'' She hesitated for a long moment, and she saw his smile die. "I can assure you that my car is clean and acceptable.''

The words came out evenly, but she knew it was happening again—him being angry—and she hated it. "I never said that.''

"No, but that's the problem, isn't it?''

"No, that's not it,'' she said quickly.

"Then what is?'' he asked, standing squarely in front of her, clearly not going anywhere until she answered him.

Heaven help her, she couldn't reveal the truth. How could she tell him that it didn't matter if he was a guard or a CEO, that the reason she couldn't take the ride from him was because he was sexy and he gave her ideas that she had no right having? "I...I don't want to bother you,'' she said, and knew how lame that sounded as soon as the words were out of her mouth. "And I'm sure you need to get back to work.''

The smile came back, a mere shadow of the former version. "I'm off now. I'm leaving. If you want to come, come on. If not...'' He leaned a bit closer.

''Call a taxi on that thing.'' He tapped her earpiece. ''And have a nice evening.''

She felt foolish and stupid, like some teenager with raging hormones. She hated the way she was aware of his throat at the open neck of his uniform shirt, of the pulse that beat there, and his slightly mussed hair. He was all male, and so damn inviting.

A ride. Just a ride. That's all this was about. ''Okay, thanks,'' she said.

''Good. Let's get going,'' he answered, and started off, back into the building and down the rear hallway. She kept pace, skipping once to keep up, and by the time they got out into the parking garage, they were side by side.

She looked at her rental car, where everything she needed was locked inside. No work tonight, except for what she could download on the computer at the loft from the company's database. ''I guess it doesn't matter leaving the car here?''

''No, it's secure.''

One slot over from her car was an oxidized blue compact that had seen better days. Right beyond it was an SUV with chrome and fancy rims. She followed Rafe toward the cars, and veered off to the passenger door of the old compact. When she looked up, she realized her mistake. Rafe was hitting an alarm button and the lights on the SUV blinked in response. She hurried past the blue car, but Rafe turned before she could totally cover her faux pas.

She didn't say a thing, but knew her face flamed. Walking quickly, she reached the SUV, where Rafe held the door open for her. As she got in, she turned, and they were at eye level for a moment, inches apart. She hated the look in those eyes. All she could do was apologize, but before she could say anything, he closed the door, hard.

She sank back in the plush leather seat, put on her seat belt and stared at her hands, resting in her lap. She heard the rattle of keys, the motor starting, and then they were moving. At the security gate, Rafe spoke, but not to her. "Diaz, leaving," he said into the speaker on the security panel.

"Did you take care of the lady at the center?" the voice asked.

"Yes, I sure did," he said.

She thought she heard the man on the other end say, "Good job," but then the security gate was raised.

They turned out of the parking garage and Megan focused on the early evening streets of Houston, and the thinning traffic. She took a breath, preparing to apologize. She couldn't leave things like this. But he spoke first.

"We'll be there in fifteen minutes," he murmured.

Fifteen minutes before he could get her out of his car and get away from her. Her hands clenched in her lap, her nails biting into her palms. "I'm sorry," she finally blurted.

He was silent for a very long time, so long that she wasn't sure he'd heard her. Maybe he was simply ignoring her. Then he cast her a glance that she couldn't read at all. His dark eyes were shadowed by the surrounding dimness, but she did see the set of his chin. He wasn't happy.

"It's nothing," he murmured.

It seemed like everything at the moment. She didn't want him to be offended or angry. She didn't know what to do to change things, but she had to try. "Rafe, I made a mistake. I assumed—"

"Yes, you did. And you were wrong."

That stung, too, and she hated that it did. "Okay, I was wrong, so why don't you shoot me like you were going to shoot that rat?"

He slowed for a light, and as the car came to a stop, he glanced at her. "I bet you thought I was stealing this when we got in it, didn't you?"

"What?"

"Got you," he said, and gave a sudden grin.

She tried to smile, to laugh, but she couldn't. She was improbably close to tears at the moment, and she didn't have any idea why. "That isn't funny," she muttered, blinking rapidly. "Not funny at all."

He gunned the car away from the light and drove in silence for a few minutes. Then he unexpectedly reached over and covered her hands with one of his. "We both need to lighten up," he said softly.

She closed her eyes tightly, feeling his warmth and strength. She stayed very still, trying to figure out why his touch was so reassuring at that moment.

Rafe felt her softness under his hand, and it felt right to just touch her. He kept the contact longer then he should have before he pulled back and gripped the steering wheel, holding on tightly to keep from touching her again. He was only vaguely aware of the way she moved a bit farther from him and spread her hands, palms down, on her thighs.

He tried to think of something to say, and ended up

doing what he didn't want to do—asking her about herself. "Didn't you say you lived in Houston before?" As soon as he said it, he wasn't sure if she'd told him that or if it had been in her personnel report. Or maybe Mary had told him. "Or did I get that wrong?"

"No, I grew up here." She named an enclave of sprawling ranches and newer estates, but when she was a kid, it would have all been ranches. Ironically, his own property was in that area.

"How big was your ranch?"

"My ranch?" she asked, seemingly taken aback that he knew the area—another thing a common security guard wouldn't know about, he thought. But there wasn't bitterness in her voice this time. "A lot of acres. My dad built it from the ground up, and he worked it until recently."

Her father worked a ranch? That didn't fit with this upwardly mobile person. "He sold it off for development?"

"Oh, no, he and my mom still own it. But my brother's going to run it, now that he's married with kids."

"Then I don't understand."

"Understand what?"

"Two things." Rafe kept his eyes straight ahead, even when she stirred in her seat and that fragrance drifted to him in the confines of the car. "Why aren't you staying there while you're in Houston, and why were you so afraid of a rat?"

"I hate rats," she said without hesitation. But she didn't answer the first part of the question. "I've always hated rats. I never understood how people made pets out of them.''

"Sort of like having a pet roach?"

She laughed softly, a wonderful sound that seemed to penetrate his being. "Yes, exactly."

"So, why aren't you staying at your ranch? Rats out there?"

"I'm sure there are. There used to be. One summer when I was a kid, maybe ten or so, I started sneaking out of the house and going to the stables. I'd climb up into the hayloft and read, and they couldn't find me. Then one day it was raining and I was curled up there reading *Pride and Prejudice,* and lightning struck. For some reason, it brought the rats out. The next thing I knew, they were running everywhere, including over my bare legs and feet." He felt her shudder. "I never did that again."

"Why did you hide out like that?" he asked, almost able to imagine her as a ten-year-old, with pale blond hair hanging in braids, and a coltish way about her.

"You won't laugh if I tell you, will you?"

"I won't laugh," he said, noticing that they were getting close to the loft area. He had to fight the urge to slow down so there'd be more time to keep her talking.

"Okay, my dad wanted me to be either a princess or a great equestrian, and since the princess thing was pretty much out unless I found a stray prince hanging around, it seemed that I had to do the horse thing."

"No other choices?"

"No, not for Dad. Unfortunately, I don't do horses. I tried it, but really didn't enjoy it. And despite the fact that almost every little girl wants a horse, and falls in love with them, I didn't. I wanted to read—far away from horses and cattle. That wasn't what Dad wanted or expected of me.''

"So you hid in the loft with your books?"

"And got attacked by an invasion of rats escaping the storm."

"Seems to me you needed a cat out there, a big, tough cat to attack anything that moved," Rafe said, and had the pleasure of hearing her laugh again.

"Touché," she murmured. "Maybe I should ship Joey out there."

"From what I've heard, he'd just be back at the loft sooner or later."

Megan saw the street for the loft and didn't know if she was relieved or disappointed. She hadn't talked to someone like this in a long time, and she'd told him about the rats, something that she'd never told anyone, not even Ryan. She had no earthly idea why she'd told Rafe any of it. "He's a stubborn cat," she said, trying to ignore where her mind was headed.

Rafe slowed when the warehouse came into sight, pulling to the curb between the old van and the three motorcycles. "Thanks," she said as soon as the car came to a full stop. "What neighbor do I ask for the key?"

"Trig. That's the name I was given."

"Just who did you call to get Trig to do this?" she asked.

"The big man, the boss," he said, and turned off the car.

"You called your boss?"

"I figured if anyone would know, he would."

"You remember when I told you about that neighbor, the one who let you in?"

"The biker?"

"That's Trig."

"Okay." Rafe was out of the car the next moment, coming around to meet her on the sidewalk, then escorting her to the warehouse entrance.

"You don't have to do this. I can take it from here," she said as she caught up with him at the call box.

He acted as if she hadn't spoken. Pressing one of the buttons on the intercom, he was greeted with a "Yeah?"

"Trig?"

"Yeah."

"Miss Gallagher from LynTech needs—"

He didn't get to finish before the harsh buzzer sounded, and when he reached for the door, she saw it open. Before she could stop Rafe from going up with her, he turned to her with one hand on the door. "I'd like to meet this guy."

Not eager to meet Trig alone again, she didn't fight Rafe going in with her and up in the elevator. When the lift stopped, he tugged up the cage door, and as they stepped out, the door to the next loft opened. Trig appeared, huge as ever, in leather pants, a vest and nothing else.

"Hey, there, little lady," he said as he came toward them. He smiled at Megan, totally ignoring Rafe. "So, you locked yourself out, did you?"

"I lost my keys," she said. "I'm sorry to bother you."

"Well, honey, I've lost keys to every place I've ever wanted to be in my life," he said with a rueful smile, then reached past her and pushed a key into the lock. It clicked and he stood back, but he didn't offer her the key. "Keys are such a boring way to get into things, don't you think?" he drawled. "But when you're in civilization, you try to be civilized, or at least give it a good shot."

"Thanks for letting me in," Megan said.

"No problem, lady." Then he casually tapped her chin, and a huge skull ring flashed on his middle finger as he lowered his voice in what she was sure he thought was a seductive tone. "Any old time you want anything, you just pucker up and whistle for Trig. You hear, sweetie?"

Rafe came closer, and she felt his sleeve brush her arm. "We've got it covered now."

Trig looked at Rafe as if surprised he was there. "You know, buddy, I can take it from here, if you'd like." He eyed Rafe's uniform. "I've done my share of bodyguard work, and if she needs one, I'd be more than glad to take over and protect her body."

Rafe wasn't a small man, but this biker made him feel dwarfed at the moment. And protective. He put his arm around Megan, and knew in some region of his mind that it felt as natural as breathing to do so. But he concentrated on the man in front of them, and didn't bother analyzing the way he startled Megan when he touched her, pulling her against his side. "Like I said, I've got it covered."

He felt Megan ease a bit closer, and her arm went around his waist, bringing their hips together. His heart skipped slightly as her heat seeped into his being, but he focused on Trig, who shrugged his massive shoulders. "Hey, I didn't know," he muttered, holding up the hand with the massive ring on it, palm toward Megan. "You and him. Who would have thought it?" Then he grinned again. "But if you throw him back, remember I'm next door, okay? No harm done?"

"No harm done," Megan said, her voice small and breathless.

"Cool," Trig said, then winked. "You two go and have fun."

Megan cringed at the suggestive words, and almost died when Rafe murmured, "That's the plan."

Chapter Nine

Rafe turned and, still holding Megan, went with her into the loft.

The minute they were inside, Megan stepped away and reached out to close the door. She stood very still, made no move to turn on any lights, and Rafe could see her in the shadows. She was softly blurred, and he could have sworn she had her ear pressed to the door. "What are you doing?" he asked.

She cut him off, whispering, "Shh, just listen."

There was no sound except for his own breathing. "What are we listening for?" he whispered back.

"For him. I never heard his door close." Then she shifted and opened the door a crack, letting a sliver of light into the darkened loft. She shut it silently again, closing out the light. "He's got his door open," she whispered, "and he's sitting right there."

"Doing what?"

She exhaled. "I don't know. He's on the floor, sitting cross-legged, with his hands on his knees, palms up, and his head back."

Rafe wouldn't mind seeing the big man like that. "I'll check it out when I leave," he said.

She spoke quickly as she threw the bolt lock on the door. "Oh no, he can't see you leave, not yet."

"Why not?"

"He thinks we're…you and me, that we're in here, and you can't just leave like that." There was a soft thump, then she moved past him and into the shadows. As he turned, a low light flashed on by the sofa. "You saw him," she whispered, coming closer again. "And he's got a key to this place. I don't want him to think I'm here alone."

Rafe was shocked that he'd never thought about that. His feelings, his emotions were blocking out all logical thought. "Okay, you're right. I should stick around for a while," he said, and just hoped she wouldn't thank him, because he was being very self-serving at that moment.

"Thank you," she said.

"But you know, this isn't in my job description."

He thought they'd laugh at least, something to break the tension, but it didn't happen. "I guess not," she said softly.

A loud thumping came at the door, and Megan jumped at the sound. Rafe moved past her, took time to undo the top two buttons on his uniform and toss the hat to one side, then opened the door. Trig was there, holding the orange cat.

"He's been squalling to get in, and it's driving us nuts," the big man said. "He's breaking up my meditation." Before Rafe could reach for the cat, the beast broke free, flying out of the biker's arms and into the loft. "Damn cat," Trig muttered, then looked past Rafe and winked. "He's all yours, sweetheart."

With that he turned and lumbered back to his place. Rafe watched him go, but the man left the door open and proceeded to sit on the floor with two others. The smell of incense was strong in the air. Rafe eased back and closed the door, then turned to find Megan standing beside him, her scent replacing the incense.

He inhaled cautiously, but still wasn't ready for the response that flooded through him as he watched her turn away from him and look up at the top of the nearest wall. He followed her gaze, and even in the shadows he could make out the dark shape of the cat.

"Great, now he's back," she murmured softly. Then she turned again, inches from Rafe. "Did Trig close the door this time?"

"No, he didn't," he said, pushing his hands into the pockets of his slacks to make very sure he didn't reach out to touch her. "It looks like they're having some sort of consciousness raising session with the help of herbs."

"Oh, great," Megan breathed, feeling caught and confined. The space in the loft seemed filled with Rafe's presence.

The evening had been crazy, her reactions to everything were even crazier. She couldn't stop thinking about his hand on hers in the car, then him pulling her to his side, protecting her from the biker. Damn it, he was just helping her, doing what he did—protecting people. It was her making so much more out of it, letting it tangle up her thoughts and touch something in her being that she couldn't begin to define.

But if he walked out now, she wasn't sure what would happen. Would Trig come on over and ask her to party? Or having a key, would he just let himself in? She didn't know why he had a key to begin with, or why he didn't give it to her. She turned away from Rafe, saying something about getting them both a drink, even though she didn't have any idea if there was anything to drink in the kitchen.

But she stopped at the kitchen door and turned back. Why couldn't she figure out if it was more dangerous for him to go, leaving her to deal with Trig, or for her to let him stay in this place with her? "Maybe you…you need to get home?" she asked. She'd forgotten about his sons. "The boys are probably waiting for you, and I can just bolt the door."

He was silent, then came across to where she stood. "A drink. I could use a drink. Any beer around here?"

Beer? "I don't think so," she said, and turned to go into the kitchen. She flipped on the overhead light, blinking at the brightness, then checked the refrigerator. Nothing to drink there except creamer. She'd used it in the last of the instant coffee that morning, and hadn't thought to go shopping.

She opened the cupboard by the small refrigerator and found the cans of tuna, and behind them, lying on its side, a bottle of wine. "Wine," she said. "How's wine?"

Rafe spoke from somewhere behind her. "Fine."

"Good," she said without looking back at him. "It's red, cabernet, so it doesn't need chilling." She reached for the drawer filled with cutlery. "Now if I can just find…'' She spotted an old-fashioned cork-screw. ''Here it is.''

She took the foil off the bottle top, then fumbled, trying to make the corkscrew work. Rafe was right behind her. ''Let me do that,'' he said, and the cork-screw fell out of her hand, clattering to the countertop.

''Sure…thanks,'' she said. Megan moved to the right, away from Rafe. ''I'll get glasses.''

She found two drinking glasses by the sink, and heard a soft popping sound. She turned and saw Rafe had opened the wine. Megan put the glasses on the counter. ''These are all I have.''

''They didn't stock the place, did they?'' he asked as he filled the glasses halfway with the dark liquid.

''I should have shopped, but I haven't had time,'' she said, reaching for the closest glass, then carrying it back to the living area.

Rafe followed, and when she crossed to the sofa, so did he. She sank down in one corner, not bothering to turn on more lights, and pushed off her shoes to tuck her feet under her. Cradling the glass in both hands, she chanced a look at Rafe. He was on the other side of the couch, looking at her as he took a sip of wine. ''So, now what?'' he asked as he lowered the glass.

''I don't know. I think you could leave soon, and as I said, I'll fasten the dead bolt. Besides, he's prob-ably harmless.'' She wasn't so sure of that, but she wouldn't admit as much to Rafe. ''And your sons are waiting for you.''

Glancing at his wristwatch, Rafe took out a cell phone and punched in a number. He spoke quickly, then closed the phone and pushed it into his pocket. "They're in bed," he said. "They're fine."

She looked down at the wine in her glass and spoke before thinking. "It must be hard without their mother."

She heard him sigh, releasing his breath softly, and she looked over at him. He was taking another drink, almost draining the glass this time. Then he was looking at her, his eyes dark and unreadable. "It was hell at first," he said softly. "I guess it was a good thing the boys were so young." He drained the last of his drink, reached for the bottle that he'd brought into the room with him, splashed it half-full again, and sat back, but didn't drink any more.

"I'm sorry, I don't know why I said that," she murmured, then took a sip of her own drink. Warmth ran down her throat, spreading in her stomach, but it didn't stop the chill she felt when she saw Rafe lean forward, his elbows on his knees. He held the glass of wine in both hands, dangling from his fingers.

"It's okay," he finally said. "It was two years ago…a lifetime away."

She took another sip, but it didn't kill the sorrow she felt deep inside her, or the desire to make things okay between them. That was foolish—beyond foolish. Her grip on the glass tightened. "I'm sorry," she finally said, not sure what else to say, and realized she'd apologized to him more often than she had to any other human being in her life.

"It seems as if I was with Gabriella all my life. We were kids when we met, and it was natural for us to get married. Then the children…" He shrugged, and his head seemed to sag. "It took forever for them to come along, and then things seemed perfect for a while."

"Was she ill for a long time?" Megan asked, not realizing that she'd moved closer to him.

"Gabriella? Sick? God, no, she was healthy as a horse. She carried the twins without a problem." He tossed back part of the wine, then closed his eyes tightly. "It was a home invasion robbery that went bad. I was working, and the boys...they were with their grandmother. Gabriella was home alone, and some punks broke in. The police think she put up a fight...she probably did...and they shot her. Just shot her and took off in her car."

Rafe exhaled, and Megan saw his shoulders shudder with the action. She moved even closer, putting her glass on the coffee table and allowing herself to touch his arm. He didn't move. He stared into his glass. There were no words, none that she could find to say to him.

"She died right away," he said. "And by the time I got there, it was over."

"Did they catch the men?"

He nodded slightly. "The next day the car was spotted, and in the chase, it crashed. One of the guys was killed, with a broken neck from being thrown from the car, and the other one...he's in prison." Rafe drank more wine, the action breaking her contact with his arm. "He's in for life."

So was Rafe, she knew. And in a fleeting moment, she felt a raging anger at the way a life could be shattered. He'd loved Gabriella. He still loved her. Megan didn't have to ask about that at all; she felt it in every word he said. "The boys…they seem so normal," she said softly, sitting beside him, but not touching him now. "So sweet."

"They're young, and as everyone tells me, kids are resilient. Too bad adults aren't," he muttered. "The twins seem to forget all about their mother—her death, anyway. Then Gabe does something like he did last week, and it all comes back. They keep saying that soon Gabriella will be like a dream to them, or a story I've been telling them."

"No," Megan said. "That won't happen. Not if you're with them. You'll keep her alive for them." She had no idea where those words came from, but they were true. She knew that. She didn't know how, but they were. "Gabriella's their mother and a part of them. She always will be," she stated, as certain of that as the fact that this man brought out things in her that she'd never known existed before.

He put his glass down on the table, then turned to her. Lifting his hand, he touched her cheek, the contact unsteady and unsettling. "Thank you," he whispered hoarsely, then he gathered her to him.

He was holding her. No, he was holding on to her, and she let him. She nestled against his chest. She felt his heart beating against her cheek, and his arms tightly surrounding her. And in that moment, she felt a jealousy for a dead woman that made no more sense to her than being here with him did.

He loved Gabriella in a way Megan had never been loved and suspected she never would be. It was that simple. Ryan was great, terrific, but there wasn't a heart-wrenching need in him to be with her. And it wasn't in her, either.

She closed her eyes tightly, trying to get a grip on reality. Then Rafe eased her back, and she was looking up at him.

The kiss that came was natural and lingering, but it wasn't passionate. It was a connection, as if Rafe needed it at that moment. He needed her to help push away the emptiness in his life.

And that was one thing she couldn't do. She wouldn't survive when he let go of her and walked away. She knew that, too.

She moved back from him, breaking the connection. He retreated in turn, reaching for the glass again, and she was suddenly alone, as surely as if he'd stood and left. That's what he had to do. He had to go. She had to figure out her feelings. And with him here, she'd never be able to do that.

She heard him take a breath, as if he was going to say something, but it got cut off when the banging sounded on the door again. Rafe stood immediately, going past her without a glance. She got up and hurried after him, and stood right behind him when he called, "Who's there?"

"It's me, buddy—Trig."

"What's going on?"

"The cat," Trig said.

Rafe glanced at her, then opened the door partway to find the huge man with the animal in his arms again. "The cat?"

"Sorry to interrupt your partying, but the cat is back and he didn't bring a hat." He grinned at Rafe as if he was pleased with his little rhyme. "Can you close off the fire escape or something, or teach him how to open it himself?"

The cat leapt out of Trig's arms, darting into the loft. "Sorry," Rafe said.

Megan turned her back to the door, watching the cat disappear into the shadows of the bedroom, and she heard Trig saying, "I don't have any food for the monster, or I think he'd be happy over there."

"I'll take care of it."

Then the door was closing, and Rafe was right behind her. She heard him say, "Megan?" softly, inches from her, but she didn't turn. She closed her eyes tightly, trying to settle herself before she faced him again.

He whispered her name again, and then his hands went around her waist. It was the fantasy she'd had, but not set in the shower. Rather, in the here and now. Slowly, he eased her back against him, and she let him. She went willingly, leaning into him, shocked at how perfectly she fit there. She closed her eyes tightly, colors exploding behind her lids as his lips found the side of her neck, the heat of his breath brushing her skin.

She felt as if he were seeping into her soul, as if they were melting into one being. He was against her, his hands flat on her stomach, pulling her into his hips, and a wave of desire flooded through her. Every inch of his body met hers, and she arched back, her head at his shoulder, as his hands skimmed up to her middle, then higher, cupping both of her breasts.

She knew what was happening, and every reason

why it shouldn't happen, but it was as if she were living the fantasy again. Touches, heat, kisses, body against body…and when she realized his hands had worked their way under her silk shirt, she was lost. His thumbs and forefingers found her taut nipples through the thin lace of her bra, and she moaned, arching more, exposing her neck to his hot kisses.

Then she turned, needing to taste Rafe, lifting her face to his, and his mouth met hers. Their groans mingled and she leaned toward him, her arms lifting to circle his neck and hold him. His kisses caused havoc, drawing out emotions that were new and stunning. She'd never wanted to get lost in another person, to let go of everything and just be. But that was exactly how she felt now as her mouth opened wider, her breasts crushed against his chest, and his hands on her bottom held her firmly against his hips.

Rafe was lost after the first touch, after reaching for her, and there was no thought of anything but feeling her, knowing her and tasting her. He didn't know why he'd told her about Gabriella, but he'd needed to. He'd had to say her name out loud, testing it, and to relate what had happened to her. He didn't understand why at all, because he hadn't spoken about it with anyone else.

Then he'd held Megan, and so many things started to happen to him. He'd kissed her, and something in him had settled—almost as if a door had closed and another had opened. It was as if the brilliance of grief had been dulled. The sharp edges were gone, and he didn't know why. Not any more than he knew why he'd reached for Megan after Trig had left again.

He tasted her, felt her heat and softness against his body, let her essence filter through him, and he knew that at least something his friends and family had told him had been right. He could move on. He could keep living. He could exist in a world where he'd known loss, but where life was still waiting for him.

He felt Megan tremble against him, and if he'd had any control up to that point, it was lost. He pushed aside her silky blouse, then her lacy bra, needing to feel skin against skin. He heard her moan when he found her hardened nipple, then her own hands were busy. She tugged at his uniform shirt, pulling it free from the waistband, fumbling with the buttons. Then her hands were on him, and his whole body responded.

Aching filled him, a need that he'd almost forgotten, and he did the only thing he could do: he picked her up in his arms. Awkwardly walking to the sofa, he sank down in the cushions with her, her body under his. He didn't know how things had gone so far, so fast, but he wasn't going to ask questions now. He felt as if he'd been given a freedom that had been denied him what seemed like forever.

Megan was the key. She was touching him, feeling his hardened desire through the taut material of his uniform slacks, and he uttered a low groan at the intense flash of feelings. He found her lips, tasted her, exploring deeply, then ran his hand along her hip to her waistband, where he fumbled with her belt.

A noise cut into the moment—a phone ringing. Not his cell phone, and not hers. It was the phone over by the workstation. Megan pushed back, fumbling to button her blouse.

"Are you going to answer it?" he asked.

She looked at him with shadowed blue eyes, and he felt his body aching. Her hair was mussed and her lips looked slightly swollen from their kisses. He didn't want her to answer the damn phone; all he wanted was her. Then the ringing stopped and the machine picked it up—an automated voice asking the caller to leave a short message after the beep.

"Megan. Ryan. Sorry to miss you, love. I got tied up, and tried to get out sooner, but you know business."

Rafe watched Megan. She wasn't moving, just staring in the direction of the phone. So that was her Ryan? "I tried your cell phone, but it wouldn't go through. I guess you're still at work. Maybe I'll try there."

Megan didn't move a muscle until Ryan lowered his voice slightly. "I miss you, babe, and sure wish you were here…" That was when Megan moved, hurrying over to the phone as Ryan kept talking. "…so we could just—"

"I'm here," she said softly.

Rafe turned from the sight of her on the phone, finished doing up his shirt, then saw Megan's cell phone on the floor by the couch. He picked it up and laid it on the side table. He turned as Megan spoke softly into the phone. "Yes, it's been too long, far too long," she said, and Rafe knew it was time to go. He'd been a fool, and his only excuse was he'd been alone too long.

He almost went out the door, but remembered Trig, and turned.

What had the biker said? Something about the fire escape? Rafe looked around, eyeing the old window system they'd used in buildings like this. He crossed to the worktable, and Megan glanced at him, the shadows hiding her eyes, but he could see the way she was clutching the phone receiver with both hands. "Yes, Ryan, yes, I do," she said, then looked away, turning her shoulder as if to shut Rafe out.

Time to go, he thought with a trace of bitterness, then headed for the fire escape. He gripped the worn metal handle, which creaked loudly as it gave and the window opened. He looked back at Megan and motioned with his hand. "I'll go out this way," he murmured. "They won't see me leave."

"No, wait," she whispered quickly.

He almost stopped, but when Ryan said something to her, she replied, "No. Of course not. It's no one."

Rafe turned away and climbed out the tall window onto a metal-railed fire escape, noting the light spilling out of the loft next door, along with the fragrance of burning herbs and the low drone of blues music. The words *It's no one* rang in his ears as he hit the release for the drop stairs, which slid out and down with remarkable quietness.

Megan was engaged, and he'd been so out of line that it made him ache. Without looking back into the loft, he climbed down, let go and jumped to the ground. He walked away into the night.

MEGAN HUNG UP from Ryan as quickly as she could, and went to the fire escape window. Rafe was gone. She buried her head in her hands for a long moment, then crossed to the front door and threw the bolt on it. After feeding the cat, she went back into the bedroom and straight through to the bathroom. At the sink, she turned on the cold water and splashed her face. A dream? A nightmare? She wasn't sure how her insanity should be labeled at that moment.

She cringed at the way she'd clung to Rafe, at the way his touch had pleasured her. And she cringed at her first reaction when she'd realized the call was from Ryan. She hadn't wanted him to phone. She hadn't wanted to hear his voice. Heaven help her, she hadn't wanted Rafe to stop. But Ryan *had* called, and the insanity had been stopped. Rafe was gone, and she was alone.

She looked in the mirror before reaching for a towel, and the eyes that looked back at her were smudged by shadows. A life that had made perfect sense to her two weeks ago made no sense now. And all because of one man.

The phone rang again, and she jumped slightly at the sound. After three rings, it went to the machine, then a voice came over the speaker, stunning her.

"Megan?" Rafe said, then waited. Finally, the dial tone came on, indicating he'd hung up.

She stood frozen at the sink, her breath caught in her throat and her hands clutching the towel. There was silence in the loft again, echoing silence. Then she pushed away from the sink and went back to the workstation. She reached for the phone, picked it up quickly and dialed Ryan's number. It rang twice, then he was on the line.

"Ryan, it's me," she said.

"Hey, I'm glad you called back. That was too brief last time."

"I need to talk," she said. "I couldn't talk last time."

"Why?"

"A man was here, and I couldn't—"

"Who was there?"

She closed her eyes tightly and knew what she had to do. After the way she'd responded to Rafe, she knew exactly what she had to do. "Ryan, we need to talk."

Chapter Ten

The next morning, Rafe had been awakened by the boys jumping on his bed and a wicked headache. He seldom drank, but last night when he'd come home he downed almost half a pint of whiskey.

Now he was at LynTech, ostensibly working on the computer to check on alarm maintenance, but was actually working off of Zane's password, going through security checks on newer employees. He was having trouble focusing on the screen because of his headache, and because of thoughts of last night.

He'd felt nothing for any woman since Gabriella died, but last night everything had exploded into a maze of confusion and need. He'd felt so much, and it had seemed such a relief—as if a dam had burst and some sort of freedom was within his reach. Then everything had shifted. Megan had withdrawn, gone back to the man she was going to marry, and Rafe had gone on alone. He still didn't know why he'd called her when he was driving away from the loft. That was crazy, and he was probably lucky she hadn't answered.

"Hey, are you going to be all day at that thing?"

He looked up to find Brad McMillan standing there, a bit flushed, even angry looking. "What's up?"

"Your job. You gotta get back out there and do the hourly check. Milt isn't coming in today, and Gus is already on the parking garage." He motioned to the computer. "Do that later."

"Sure," Rafe said, careful to get out of the secured program before leaving the terminal, and trying to ignore Brad's commanding tone. He stood, flexed his shoulders and winced at his headache. "Do you know if they have some sort of nurse or something in the building?"

"What's going on?" Brad asked, his eyes narrowing.

"A headache. I just need an aspirin or something."

"Oh," he said. "A hard night?"

"Very hard," Rafe admitted.

"Anything to do with that ice princess I sent on down to you last night? Although it beats me why I was helping you. I stand to lose a ton if you get anywhere with her."

"Too much whiskey," Rafe said.

"Oh, too bad." The security guard grinned. "You're gonna strike out, buddy."

"Probably am," Rafe muttered. "Now, the aspirin?"

"Yeah, they got stuff like that at the day care center. They've got a first aid kit. Just ask that old lady, Mary something or other, and she'll take care of you."

"Thanks," Rafe said, and stepped around Brad to head down to the center. He would check on the boys while he was at it. He turned as he left the computer area, and saw Brad slipping into his seat. The other man looked up, frowned and said, "Get going."

Rafe did exactly that, heading for the elevators and down to the center. When he walked in, the place seemed empty, until he went farther into the main room and he saw the teenager who had been there earlier. She was sorting through books and looked up when she heard him. "Hi there, Mr. Diaz," she said.

Hearing his mother's maiden name still seemed weird to Rafe. But it was necessary in order to keep up the cover. "Where is everyone?"

"On a field trip to the dairy. Cows and things," she said, with a bit of a grin. "The babies are in the quiet room napping."

"Okay," he said, realizing the twins had been saying something about that on the way in today, but he'd been preoccupied. "I was told there's a first aid kit around here somewhere?"

"Sure," she said, and motioned beyond the tree. "In Mrs. Garner's office, on the shelf right by the door. You can't miss it."

He thanked her and headed for the office. The door was open and he started to go inside, but stopped when he saw Megan working at the desk, intent on papers spread out in front of her. He watched her quietly for a moment, the way she leaned forward, exposing the nape of her neck. Her hair was caught back in a low twist, revealing a flash of gold—earrings. Watching her, Rafe could barely breathe.

He'd thought last night was madness, but at least a passing madness. Now he knew he couldn't even look at her without wanting her. But he wasn't going to get her... He would have turned and left if she hadn't looked up right then. If she hadn't met his gaze with her improbable blue eyes, and if her pink lips hadn't parted softly in surprise. A flush of color crept into her cheeks.

She sat back slowly, but didn't look away. She didn't say anything at all, just watched him. He knew he had to speak. "Hello."

Sparkling dialogue, he thought miserably, while his head throbbed.

"Hi," she murmured, then let him off the hook. "Were you searching for Mary?"

For a moment he'd forgotten why he'd come, then recovered. "No, just looking for the first aid kit."

Megan seemed to straighten in the chair. "Why, is something wrong?"

Yes, everything, he thought to himself, but actually said, "Nothing serious." He looked to his right and found the kit. He retrieved two aspirin and sighed with relief. "Perfect," he said, and closed the box, then put it back in its place.

"Are you sick?" she asked.

He glanced at her. "No, I'm not sick, just a bad headache." He let his gaze skim over her features, and felt his whole body begin to tighten. "So, did Trig leave you alone last night?"

"Mary Garner knows the daughter of the man who used to own that loft—the hippie? And she said that Trig is really a CEO of some corporation in Colorado. He does the biker thing for relaxation. I mean, the man is worth millions and he wears that ugly leather vest, and rides a hog, or whatever they call those big bikes."

"A CEO named Trig?"

"Mary said that he got that name because he's some sort of genius at math. Isn't that remarkable?"

What was remarkable was the way her whole face had softened and her eyes were glowing with delight. Obviously she was relieved that a killer biker wasn't living next door. "Very remarkable," he said.

"So he's okay."

"Are you reconsidering letting him be your body-guard?" Rafe asked, and the instant the words were out, she blushed.

"He's just a nice guy," she said, then changed the subject. "Mary had my keys, by the way. She took them home with her accidentally. So everything's just fine."

It wasn't fine for Rafe. Not at all. He'd finally figured out there was life out here for him, had finally realized that Megan stirred that life, but now he knew she couldn't be part of it. That wasn't fine. Not even close. "Yeah, just fine," he said, the headache making his eyes slightly blurry.

He thought she was frowning at him, but her face was a soft blur now. "Are you sure you're okay?" she asked.

"The headache," he said, and held up the aspirin in his hand. "Just the headache." He turned to leave, but she stopped him when she said his name.

"About last night, I was..." She spoke softly, her words trailing off, and he wasn't at all sure that he'd heard her correctly.

He swallowed hard, but didn't look back. "Feed the cat, and keep your fire escape exit locked," he said, then walked out.

Megan sank back into the chair, trying to make her heart stop hammering in her chest. She hadn't wanted to talk about Trig or the damn cat, but it was easier than discussing what had happened between them. The long hours after he'd left had been strange and disturbing, with little sleep and many unanswered questions.

It had been so hard to talk to Ryan once Rafe had left. The words had come haltingly, but she'd known what had to be said.

"We need to talk."

"We sure do," he'd said softly.

No, that wasn't what she wanted. This man deserved more. "Ryan, can you come out here for a day so we can talk in person?"

"Don't tempt me. But with the business so crazy right now, it's just not possible."

"Oh," she said softly.

"Is something wrong?"

She closed her eyes for a moment, then opened them as she caught the phone between her shoulder and her ear. She touched the engagement ring, then slipped it off. "Yes, something's very wrong."

There had been silence, then a single word. "What?"

She took a breath, then laid the ring on the desk and said, "We can't get married." The words had hung there, and she hadn't been able to take them back. And more importantly, she hadn't wanted to. She sighed at the memory, sadness lingering still, but she'd done the right thing for both of them.

Rafe was there, in her life, good or bad. He was a

stranger who was as lonely as she was, or maybe lonelier. He was also a guard with two little boys, a man she didn't know existed two weeks ago, but suddenly none of that mattered. None of it. She knew him now, and there was something there. Something that shouldn't be if she loved Ryan enough to marry him. With Ryan, those feelings hadn't been there; they never would be.

"Megan?"

Her thoughts interrupted, she looked up to find Mary coming into the office. "It's noon already?" she asked.

"No, I had to come back early…to talk to someone." She looked bothered, but made a dismissive motion with her hand, then smiled a bit weakly. "How are things here?" She glanced at the papers. "How did we do with the ball?"

"From what I can tell," she said, thankful to have something simple to focus on, "with Accounting's figures, if they're verified, you did very well. The hospital will be grateful, and the center will have enough funding to begin plans for expansion."

"That's wonderful," Mary said as she came around the desk. "Just wonderful."

The phone rang, and Mary reached for it. "Just For Kids."

Megan gathered her things together, ready to head back up to Legal.

As Megan stood and Mary took the chair, the older woman said, "What?"

Megan glanced down at her, and saw the blood drain out of her face. "Oh, yes. Yes. I'll take care of that. Where did they take him?'' She grabbed a pen and scribbled on a scrap of paper. ''Tell them to do everything they can, and I'll get his parent.''

''What's wrong?'' Megan asked as Mary started dialing another number.

''It's one of the twins—Greg. He's been hurt.''

Megan stared at the woman. ''But they went to a dairy, didn't they?''

Mary was on the phone again pushing in numbers, then said, ''Yes. Greg fell and they've taken him to—'' The explanation was cut off abruptly. ''This is Mary Garner at the day care center. I need to contact Rafe Diaz immediately. It's an emergency.'' She listened for a moment. ''Find him, and have him get down here or call me right away,'' she said, and hung up.

All Megan could think of was how much the boys meant to Rafe. He'd lost their mother, and there was no way he could go through losing a child, too. ''He was just here ten minutes ago.''

''They said he's on rounds, and they're going to try and page him, or send someone to look for him.'' Mary sank back in the chair, her complexion still pale. ''Oh, my,'' she breathed. ''That poor baby.''

Megan left her papers on the desk, grabbed her purse and started for the door. ''I'll find him,'' she said.

She ran out of the office, through the center, then out into the lobby of the building. Brad McMillan was at the front door, and she pushed past a group of people that had just gotten off the elevator and hurried over to him. ''Where's Mr. Diaz?''

''That's what I'd like to know,'' he muttered.

"Everyone's looking for him. What do you need with him?"

She ignored the strident question and turned, running to the back exit, and out into the parking garage. His car was still there. He wasn't in the guard station at the security gate. She started to turn to go back inside, but stopped when the door to a private elevator that went straight up to the executive level opened and Rafe burst out.

One look at his face and she knew that he knew. "Rafe!" she called, and met him halfway between his car and the elevator. "They got in touch with you?"

He looked at her as if she was speaking a foreign language, then seemed to focus slightly. "Yes," he said, and broke away from her, heading for the car.

She ran after him, and when she saw him try to manipulate the alarm release, she reached out and took it from him. "Get in. I'll drive."

He had the keys back in his hand before she could react. "I'll drive," he said, and the doors opened.

She ran around and barely got in the passenger side before Rafe had started the car and headed for the security gate. The tires squealed slightly as he braked, reached out the window, punched in a code. She thought for a minute he was going to ram the gate, trying to get out before it was up all the way, but he managed to just clear it as he drove up the ramp and out onto the street.

Megan held the armrest on the door, her other hand clutching the edge of the seat as Rafe wove through traffic, hitting several lights too close to the red.

"Damn," he muttered under his breath when the traffic up ahead started to slow.

Before Megan knew what he was going to do, he made a sharp right turn into an alleyway, shot through it, with the huge car barely clearing the sides, then burst out onto the next street. Thankfully, there was a gap in the traffic, and the SUV skidded, turned left and accelerated up the street.

"You...you have to slow down," Megan gasped when he barely missed sideswiping a car in the left lane.

He didn't act as if he'd heard her, but she saw the way his hand gripped the gearshift and his knuckles whitened.

"You won't be any good to the boys if you get hurt," she said.

The words must have gotten through, because he slowed slightly, easing back just a bit. But he never looked at her. "What did Mary tell you?" he asked in a low, tight voice, his eyes determinedly focused as he made a tight right turn.

"Just that Greg was hurt."

She thought she heard him say, "Oh, God," but the words were all but obliterated when a horn sounded as Rafe cut in front of a slower car and shot through a light just before it turned red.

Then she saw the hospital ahead of them, the sun glinting off the banks of windows in the huge complex. There was a squeal of tires as Rafe hit the turn into the E.R. parking lot. He skidded to a stop by an idling ambulance, then turned off the engine and leapt out, running toward the entrance. Megan scrambled out after him, ignoring someone yelling that they couldn't park there.

When she got into the emergency room, she saw Rafe talking to a white-coated doctor. "Where is he?" Rafe demanded.

The man checked a clipboard in his hands, and as Megan reached them, she heard the doctor say, "Bed ten." He glanced at Megan, then back at Rafe before he motioned to a door behind them. "I'll ring you in."

He went to a security pad by the door, punched in a code, and the door buzzed. Rafe hit the handle, and when the door swung back, Megan followed him into the E.R., past cubicle after cubicle hidden behind pulled curtains. The sound of beeping monitors, all out of sync with each other, seemed to be everywhere. Rafe strode down the aisle, then stopped and pulled back a curtain.

Gabe all but leapt out of the arms of one of the day care center's staff and into his dad's. He hugged Rafe for dear life, burying his face in his chest. Then Megan saw Greg. The child was lying very still in the bed, his skin pale and his eyes closed. A stark white bandage covered almost his entire forehead.

Rafe held Gabe, but moved to Greg, reaching out to touch his son's hand. "Greg?" he said in a low, unsteady voice. "Buddy boy?"

The little boy stirred, opened his eyes, then focused on his father's face, his relief heart-wrenching. "Daddy," he whispered, and Rafe bent over him, holding Gabe and hugging Greg at the same time.

Finally he stood back and looked at the woman who had been sitting with Gabe when they came in. Megan had recognized her as a part-time worker at the center. "What happened?" he asked.

"Sir, I'm so sorry. He just moved so quickly. He got in a stall while a cow was being milked, and he tried to climb up and ride it." She looked so worried. "Now that you're here, I really need to get back to the center."

Rafe thanked her, then looked back at Greg. "You tried to ride a cow?"

"Huh," the tiny boy said. "He was real big and brown, sort of." He grimaced. "But I couldn't. He wouldn't let me. I hurted my head real bad."

Megan saw the tension in Rafe, and could only begin to imagine how he felt right then, seeing his child in a hospital bed. Her heart ached with sympathy. When he shifted Gabe to his other arm, she found herself touching him on the shoulder.

"Rafe?"

He darted her a quick look. "You can leave," he said, without giving her a chance to say anything.

"No, no," she said. "Let me take Gabe?"

He hesitated, probably as surprised as she was by her offer. She knew she didn't have many maternal instincts, but right then she felt an overwhelming need to do something to help make the situation easier for Rafe. "He's okay," Rafe finally said, but Gabe overrode his words by twisting toward Megan, his hands stretched out.

A second later the little boy was in her arms, and without hesitation, snuggled into her shoulder, burying his face in her neck. She adjusted him on her hip and softly patted his back, never looking away from Rafe.

''It's okay,'' she said, as much for his sake as for the child's.

Rafe closed his eyes for a long moment, then his dark eyes met hers again. ''I need to go and find the doctor.''

''Go ahead. I'll stay here.''

But he didn't have to leave. A doctor pulled back the curtains right then. ''I'm Dr. Wynn.'' He held out his hand to Rafe. ''You must be Greg's dad.'' The two men shook hands, then the doctor turned to Megan. ''And you must be Greg's mom.''

Rafe literally braced himself for the blow he knew would come with the doctor's words, but incredibly, it didn't materialize. He had a flat feeling in his middle, an oddly detached sensation, then a sense of settling that he didn't understand. But what he understood completely was the image of Megan holding Gabe to her, cuddling him to her shoulder and watching Rafe carefully with those huge blue eyes. She didn't say a thing.

''How's Greg?'' Rafe finally asked.

The doctor, a nice man with faded blue eyes and thinning black hair, actually smiled. ''Oh, he's a tough kid. No real damage done, beyond two stitches and some bruises.'' He moved closer and leaned over his patient while he kept talking to Rafe. ''He's going to have a scar, but there are no signs of concussion or anything.'' Then he straightened and looked back at Rafe. ''You can take your son home now, but my advice is to keep him away from cows until he's older. Have that wound looked at in a few days by his own doctor.''

The relief Rafe felt registered on so many levels that it made him slightly light-headed. He knew he thanked the doctor, but later he couldn't have told anyone what words he'd used. He didn't remember picking up Greg, but he remembered having to take several deep breaths to steady himself before he looked at Megan again. She smiled, a soft upward curl of her lips, and asked, "He was trying to ride a cow?"

He felt Greg hug him and snuggle closer. "A cowboy fixation," he murmured, then nodded to Gabe. "Can you manage him? He can get pretty heavy."

"I knew I took those weight lifting classes at the gym for something," she said, her smile growing wider as she shifted the little boy on her hip. "I'm fine."

She didn't look particularly athletic, but rather slender and delicate. "Good," he said. Then the four of them headed back through the E.R. and out into the noontime sun. That's when Rafe stopped and stared in disbelief at a red-and-white ambulance that was parked right where his car had been. "What in the—?"

He looked around, certain this was where he'd left the SUV, then saw a guard off to one side and called out to him.

The man came toward him, and Rafe could see he was wearing a Dagget Security uniform, including a badge and a name tag that read "S. Smits."

"What do you need?" the man asked. Then he saw Rafe's uniform. "Hey, you work for the company?"

"Yes, but I'm over at LynTech. My son was just in the E.R. and I parked my car here." He motioned with his head toward the ambulance. "Now it's gone."

"A black SUV?"

"That's the one," Rafe said.

The man looked at Megan and Gabe, then back at Rafe and Greg. "Sorry, buddy, but we tow in restricted zones."

Rafe knew that, and if the guy followed the rules, the next thing he'd do would be to give Rafe a card with the address of the impoundment yard on it and the phone number to call to get the car back. After that, a short sermon on violating a restricted parking zone would have been appropriate. "Can you call and get it back here?" he asked without much hope. He couldn't pull rank. Not here, not now.

"Wish I could, buddy, professional courtesy and all, but I don't think—"

"Sir?" Megan said, and the guard turned to her. "It's been hard enough going through everything in the E.R., but this is so disturbing, and the twins need to get home as quickly as possible."

"Ma'am, I understand, and if it was just up to me, I'd do it in a minute, but..." He shrugged. "Sorry."

Then Megan smiled at the guard. It was a slightly sad expression, but laced with understanding. "Oh, I know—it's your job and you can't do anything to jeopardize it. I'm sorry for asking. I shouldn't have, but I was just hoping..." She let her voice trail off as she readjusted Gabe in her arms. "Never mind, we understand."

"Oh, man, I could get in a heck of a lot of trouble,

but…okay, okay.'' He glanced at Rafe, then at Megan. ''I'll get that car back for you.''

Rafe didn't know if he should laugh or be ticked off that the man could be bribed, even if that bribe was a smile that he knew few men could resist.

''Oh, thank you so much,'' Megan said with an even sweeter smile. Rafe wondered if she had any idea how her smile affected people, but found out she probably did when the guard looked away to take out his two-way radio, and her smile grew larger as she met Rafe's gaze.

He found himself returning the smile and barely controlling a laugh. He looked away from her to the guard, and focused on the man speaking into the radio. ''Spike? The SUV you got on the back of your truck? Bring it on back to the E.R. entrance.'' There was static, a voice that he couldn't make out, but the guard obviously could. ''It was a mistake and I'll take the heat. Just bring it on back here, right away.'' Then the man looked at Megan again. ''It'll just be a few minutes, ma'am, but it's on its way back.''

''Oh, thank you so much,'' she breathed. ''You're terrific.''

The man actually seemed to blush a bit. ''It's nothing, but I need to get on with my rounds. Now, if you have any problem at all, you go inside and tell them to radio Sly Smits. That's me.''

''I just don't know how to thank you, Sly,'' she murmured, her chin resting on Gabe's head.

''No need,'' the man said, then took off.

Rafe moved closer to Megan and leaned down to speak to her in a low voice. ''Nice job, Counselor. If

I ever need representation, I'll be sure to bring you into court with me.''

''Oh, he wanted to do the right thing,'' she said, those blue eyes turned up to his and that smile lingering in their depths. ''Most people do.'' Rafe bet that smile of hers was illegal in any number of states. ''I just hope he doesn't get in any trouble over this.''

''He won't,'' Rafe said, and knew that he couldn't fault the man for giving in when Megan smiled. ''But you have to get back to work, don't you?''

She shifted Gabe a bit, let him settle with a sigh, then said, ''It's okay. Mary probably figured out why I left and where I went, so she can tell Mr. Lawrence where I am.''

''Well, if you need to get going, we'll be fine,'' he said. That was a lie, but he had to offer.

She shook her head as she slowly patted Gabe's back. ''I came in your car, remember?'' Before he could respond, she glanced past him. ''And there it is.''

He turned at the sound of a heavy diesel engine, and saw a black-and-white tow truck lumbering toward them with his car hitched behind. Both boys were immediately alerted by the sound. ''Daddy, it's got our car,'' Greg exclaimed.

''Sure does,'' Rafe said, watching as the truck stopped, and a man got out to lower and undo the SUV from the chains. He finally came around to Rafe. ''Is this your car?''

''Yes, it is.''

''Next time, don't park it in a restricted area.''

''Absolutely not.''

With that, the man got back in the truck and drove off, while Rafe and Megan carried the boys to the SUV and secured them in their safety seats. Rafe got in behind the wheel and watched Megan climb into the passenger seat. For a second, he had the same flash as he had in the E.R. room—fantasies about what might be. But wouldn't be. He reined in those fantasies, foolish and frustrating as they were, when he glanced at the ring on her finger. Totally useless. "Let's get out of here," he murmured, and put the car into gear.

Chapter Eleven

They drove in silence most of the way, at least until Rafe sensed Megan looking back at the boys. "They're asleep," she said in a soft voice.

"They're worn out," Rafe said, releasing a deep breath.

"Are you going to take them straight home?"

He glanced at them in the rearview mirror. "Yes." He took out his phone, then put in a call to Carmella, and quickly told her what had happened. After reassuring her that both boys were fine, he asked if she could come back to the house early today. She didn't hesitate to agree. "We'll be there in a bit," he said, and hung up.

He laid the cell phone on the console. "The babysitter's meeting me at the house."

"They'll let you off for the day, don't you think? I mean, it being a family emergency and all."

He knew that rule wasn't in the employment contract his employees signed. "No, it doesn't work that way."

"It should."

"How do you think it should work?"

"Anyone deserves time off when a child's been hurt or is sick. They need to have a parent with them."

He'd make sure that change was put into effect when he called the head office later to make sure the guard at the hospital didn't get into any trouble. "Okay, I'll mention it to somebody and see what happens. Why don't you call Mrs. Garner and let her know what's going on?"

She did as he asked, while Rafe listened. "I'm with Mr. Diaz now. He's dropping me back at work, then he's taking the boys home." Megan listened again, laughed softly, then said, "I'll see you soon," and hung up. She turned the phone off, then looked at him. "She pretty much figured out where I was, and she said to tell Greg to get better soon."

"I'll let him know when he wakes up," Rafe said, and turned onto the street where LynTech was located. He rolled up to the curb at the front of the building, waved off the valet who started toward his car, then checked on the boys before he turned in the seat to look at Megan. "Back to work for you," he said.

She seemed to hesitate, then touched his hand where it rested on the console next to his phone. "Are you okay?"

The three words were filled with concern and, combined with her touch, made his throat tighten. "Sure, I'm fine now," he said, and heard the roughness in his own voice. "Thanks for asking."

Her hand tightened on his for a moment, then the connection was gone. "Do you want me to tell Security what's going on, or anything?"

He glanced past her and saw Brad through the glass door. "Send the door guard out for a minute, and I'll explain."

"Sure." She glanced back at the boys one last time, then got out and hurried toward the doors. He watched her head inside, and before long Brad was jogging toward the car. Rafe rolled down his window.

"Heard what happened," Brad said. "Kids sure mess up your life, don't they?"

Brad obviously didn't have a clue what Rafe's boys meant to him. "They make it interesting. I just wanted you to know I'd be gone a while."

"No problem. Word came down a few minutes ago that you have today off and whatever other time you need." He grimaced slightly. "I don't know who you know, but they're handing you a deal, buddy."

"I'll take it." At least for the rest of today. When he expected Brad to move away and let him leave, the man leaned in the window. "So, you got her in the car, huh?" He glanced at the wedding ring. "Not that I'd tell anyone or say anything." He winked conspiratorially. "You're scaring me. You might just win this thing."

Rafe felt his distaste of Brad rise to a new level. "She was just helping me at the hospital."

He raised one eyebrow. "Helping you with what?" Then he hit Rafe on the arm. "Forget it, buddy. You've got another week." This time he hit the frame of the window. "Get out of here."

Rafe nodded and drove off, glad to be away from the man. As he wove through the city streets, heading toward the ranch, Brad faded from his thoughts, and

Megan took over. Fantasies formed, but Rafe let them go. An ice princess? No, she wasn't cold. She wasn't severe and remote, the way Brad had her pegged. Rafe knew that. And he knew how wrong he'd been about her at first. At least partially. He couldn't quite forget their conversation that night at the loft.

He'd told her about Gabriella, and it had seemed the right thing to do. It had been a relief to him, saying things he hadn't said to anyone since she died. Then everything had changed with the phone call at Megan's loft, the night they'd almost made love. *It's no one.* He was nobody. At least Rafe, the hourly guard, was nobody. And he couldn't tell her who he really was. Not yet.

Then again, she'd stayed with him, helped him with the boys, when she'd been the one to tell him once that she wasn't good with kids. He'd always been afraid to feel anything for anyone since Gabriella had gone. In a way, being with another woman seemed dishonest. Or maybe the hurt, the pain of possibly losing someone else, wasn't worth it. He'd barely survived losing Gabriella. How could he ever go through that again?

But with Megan things were different. He wasn't sure where this…relationship was going, if anywhere, but he couldn't just walk away. He wouldn't.

AT WORK THE NEXT DAY, and over the weekend, Megan fought the urge to call Rafe and make sure everything was okay. She'd heard from Mary that Greg was doing fine, that Rafe was with him. She wanted to know for herself. But she never made that call, and instead worked straight through the weekend at the loft.

By the time she went to work on Monday, she was on edge. She worked on the computer at the center all day, but didn't see Greg. No Gabe. No Rafe. Mary wasn't sure why they hadn't come in, but didn't seem concerned. Then late in the afternoon, she came into the office.

Megan looked up when Mary spoke. "I'm not finished with the document," she said.

"Oh, I didn't expect them this soon."

"Well, Mr. Lawrence expects a rough report before I leave," she said, sitting back.

"That man works you too hard."

"It's okay," she said, and meant it. Working kept her thoughts occupied, because when she wasn't focusing on work, her mind drifted into the strangest scenarios. Most of them involving Rafe. "I'll get them to you tomorrow."

"Fine, fine."

"Did you need something?"

"I was just wondering if you'd heard anything from Mr. Diaz?"

Megan pressed her hands flat on the papers on the desk. "No. Why?"

"Just wondering. He didn't call today, and I haven't seen him." She reached for the phone caddy on the desk, flipped through the cards, then pulled one free. "Here," she said, offering it to Megan. "Why don't you give him a call and see when he's bringing the boys back? The other children are asking for the twins."

Megan took the card and looked at it, then back at Mary. "I don't want to bother him."

"Please, just call. I'd do it, but I'm meeting someone and I can't be late."

"The children are all gone?"

"The last two just left. Brittany picked up Walker and Anthony. So you'll have peace and quiet."

She actually hadn't noticed the noise lately. It just sort of blended into the background. She fingered the card. "Okay, I'll call."

"Leave me a note if there's a problem?"

"Sure."

"Well, I'm off. You have a good evening, and don't work too much longer. It's not good for a young woman like you." Then she left, and Megan read the number on the card.

She put in the call, closing her eyes as it rang once, twice, before it was answered. "Yes?" a woman asked in soft voice.

"I'm calling from the day care center at LynTech. We were wondering about the twins, when they'll be back?"

"I'm sorry, they're not here, and I'm not sure when Mr. Rafe expects to bring them back to the center."

"Thanks. I just wanted to make sure they were okay."

"Oh, they're fine. Just fine."

"Thanks a lot," she said, and hung up.

It was then she realized that she had wanted Rafe to answer the phone so she could hear his voice. Megan shook her head sharply, then started to gather up the papers to put in her briefcase. She was done. At least she had the work Mr. Lawrence needed first thing in the morning. She'd finish the rest at the loft. She put everything away, picked up her briefcase and headed up to Legal to get the rest of her things and leave the folder for her boss.

She went straight to her cubicle there, found a big envelope and slipped Mr. Lawrence's papers in it, then headed for his office. She knew he was gone. In fact, everyone was gone. She went through the empty offices, into Mr. Lawrence's private office and put the folder on his desk. She found a pen, wrote, "Revised Figures for Charity Ball," signed her name, added the time and date, then turned to leave.

Time stopped the moment she found Rafe in the doorway. He was in his uniform, with no hat, those dark eyes lost in the shadows. "Oh," she breathed softly when she found her breath.

"Hi, there." He didn't move. "How are you?"

"Just leaving papers for my boss."

"I asked how you are, not what you're doing," he said, and the suggestion of a smile touched his lips.

"Oh, I'm doing just fine," she said, staying where she was. "How's Greg?"

"Great. He'll have a scar, and he's pretty proud of it."

"They gave you time off?"

He nodded. "All the time I needed. I just came back today because they were shorthanded."

"But the boys weren't in the center."

"They're with family for a day or two." He leaned one shoulder against the door frame and crossed his arms on his chest. She saw his wedding band gleam in the overhead light. Then she looked at him, and knew that he'd noticed where she'd been looking. "How's your job going?" he asked.

"It's going well," she said, and picked up her briefcase, ready to leave, except that he was blocking the doorway.

"Any idea if you'll get that promotion?"

She shook her head and told him truthfully, "I don't know yet."

He still didn't make a move to leave or let her pass. "How's the cat?"

"He comes and goes, and does whatever he wants to do."

"And Trig, the genius biker?"

"He's gone. He took off with his friends yesterday, heading back to Colorado and, I assume, the boardroom."

"You never can tell from first impressions, can you?"

"No, you can't."

He looked at her intently for a long moment, then said, "Ready?"

"Yes."

When she went by him, she felt his uniform sleeve brush her arm, but she kept going. He fell in step beside her, silently keeping pace with her. But when she would have stopped at the elevators, he said, "They're turned off for maintenance. It's the stairs or nothing."

"Okay," she murmured, and headed down the hallway to the stairs. When she reached the door, she went into the stairwell and started down, more aware than ever of Rafe's presence. As they went down in silence, she felt him watching her. "Is something wrong?" she finally asked as they approached the last series of stairs before reaching the ground floor.

"No," he said, and kept going. But when he hit the bottom landing, he turned, and she stopped two stairs above where he stood. He stared at her bare ring finger, then at her face, and said, "You know what?"

All she could think about was the memory of being in his arms at the loft. The feel of his body along hers, his hands on her, his kiss and taste. "Uh, no, what?" she managed to say.

"I hate this."

She hated it, too. She hated remembering so much about him, but at that moment, if she'd had to recall her first kiss with Ryan, she couldn't have. "You hate what?"

"This hedging and game playing."

Ever since they'd met, she'd felt it was a game of some sort, but the stakes were higher than she'd ever imagined. "What do you mean?"

"Small talk, acting as if we're passing strangers who haven't ever..." His voice trailed off, but she knew what he meant. Thankfully, he didn't put it into words. Instead he said, "I'm acting as if I ran into you by accident in Legal. The truth is, I tracked you down. I've been looking for you for more than fifteen minutes, and thought you might have already left." He narrowed his eyes. "Can I be honest with you?"

Her heart was hammering and she almost couldn't breathe, but she managed to nod, because she couldn't have spoken then to save her life.

"I'm out of practice with women, and I'm not sure

how to do it." He smiled ruefully, a smile that was so damn endearing it only made things worse for her. "But I'm willing to give it a shot."

"You were looking for me?" she asked, shocked that she was asking that when so many other questions were floating around in her mind.

He came up a step and it put them on eye level with each other, with no more than three inches separating their bodies. He touched the railing on either side of her, surrounding her, yet not touching her. "Yes, I was."

"Oh," she whispered.

"Yes, oh," he breathed. He hesitated, then she saw him take another breath. "Will you have dinner with me tonight? Just friends, going to dinner. I'm off work, and you're here and I'm here." He shrugged slightly. "How about it?"

There were so many reasons to say no to his questions, so many sensible reasons, and she tried to be sensible.

He nodded toward her hand and she realized she was rubbing the place where the ring had been. "I won't ask where your ring is. This will just be dinner and talk, and if at the end of the evening, that's it, I won't fight it." He smiled a bit uncertainly. "Dinner. Food. Talking. That's it." He drew back, making a crossing motion over his heart. "Promise."

She exhaled, and knew she wanted to go with him, to talk to him, to just be there. "Okay, I'll go."

She told him she'd meet him by his SUV while he went and changed out of his uniform. Meanwhile she made herself breathe, in and out, easy and deep, trying to settle herself. And she almost managed to do it, until she turned and saw Rafe coming out of the executive elevator across the space.

He was wearing a silky, short-sleeved white shirt with no collar, making his tan look deeper, more coppery. Black slacks were molded to his hard thighs and set off his lean hips. He'd brushed his hair straight back from his face. When he saw her, he smiled, and the expression made her swallow hard. He was so attractive. No, not just attractive, he was as sexy as hell. And she felt heat flood through her as he got close, making her turn and go to the passenger door.

"I should have changed," she said as she climbed into the SUV, but Rafe turned to face her, slowly taking in her navy linen slacks and off-white silk blouse.

Then those dark eyes met hers. "I'd say you look perfect." He started the car and drove out of the structure and onto the evening streets. She watched him as he drove, and he spoke without looking at her. "The executive elevator's on a separate control panel."

"Excuse me?"

"I thought you were wondering about me coming out of the elevator when I told you they weren't working."

"Oh," she said, not about to tell him she was actually wondering how he could be so distracting, when all he was doing was driving the car. "And your clothes?"

"I keep a change at work, just in case." He flashed her a glance accompanied by an easy smile. "I've just never had a reason to change before."

She pressed her hands against the briefcase on her

lap and for a moment missed her engagement ring. Ryan's grandmother's ring. It had been heavy on her finger. She covered her bare finger with her right hand and bit her bottom lip. She looked away from Rafe, out at the city around them, and felt removed from the real world. But stunningly, not alone. Not lonely at all. And she settled in the seat, letting the feeling wash over her, for now. Then the car slowed and she realized they were in a very upscale area of the city, and stopping at the valet parking of a restaurant she'd been to years ago. A very expensive restaurant she'd gone to with her brother, Quint, and his grown son.

She looked over at Rafe as he got out of the SUV, while she was helped from her seat when the attendant opened her door. Rafe took a ticket from the valet, then was by her side, touching her lightly on the elbow. But she didn't move. He looked at her. "Is something wrong?" he asked.

"Can we…can we talk?" she asked in a voice just above a whisper. The last thing she wanted to do was embarrass him in front of the attendant.

"We can talk inside," he said, but she stood her ground.

She looked past him toward some stone benches for customers waiting for their cars to be brought around. "Over there?" she asked, pointing to them.

He hesitated, then went with her, but he didn't sit down. He turned to face her. "What's wrong?" he asked, his eyes narrowed and wary.

"This place," she said in a low voice, leaning toward him to keep the conversation just between the two of them.

"You don't like good food?"

"Of course I do, but—"

"Then what's the problem?"

"It's very expensive," she finally said, and let the words hang between them.

"I know," he answered simply.

"But you don't understand, this is *expensive*. The appetizers are over thirty dollars each. And you can forget about wine. It's all cellared and it's—"

He reached out and touched her lips with his forefinger, stopping her words midsentence. "I know," he said. "And it's okay." His finger trailed slowly over her bottom lip before he drew back. "Can we go in now?"

"We can go Dutch," she blurted.

That brought a soft laugh from him, then he murmured, "That won't be necessary. Trust me."

Before she could say anything else, he slipped his arm around her shoulders and headed inside. They were greeted by a man in a modified tuxedo, effusively welcoming them to La Porte D'or. They were lead into a private area with tables discreetly camouflaged from each other by strategically placed potted palms and ornate screens. In a room beyond, a pianist softly played old favorites.

Megan took the red velvet, high-backed chair that the host held out for her, then she sat facing Rafe. He accepted the wine list, scanned it, then looked at her. "Any preference in wine?"

She wanted to say, "Something really cheap," but just shook her head.

He put in an order for a good merlot that she knew

was mid-range in price, costing what he probably made in a week, and her discomfort only grew. Then the host was gone, and Rafe looked across at her. "Relax. You'll love the food here."

She knew she would. She'd been here before. But that didn't change the fact that he was spending more money than anyone should, and she couldn't just sit back and let him do it. "Rafe, I'm not sure about this."

He glanced at where her engagement ring had been, where she pressed her left hand to the white of the linen tablecloth. "Are you sure about the engagement?" he asked.

She drew her hand back, not about to explain herself to him—not now. "What does that mean?"

The wine steward appeared with the wine selection. Rafe tested it, nodded, and the man filled their goblets. Rafe lifted his and said, "To the best-laid plans."

She couldn't even reach for her glass. "Rafe, stop."

He put his glass down, the wine untouched. "Stop what?"

"I was wrong. I don't think we should do this."

"Do what?"

She motioned vaguely around them. "This. Any of it."

He sat forward, rolling the stem of the fine crystal slowly back and forth with his thumb and forefinger. "Why don't you explain that to me."

She shrugged, then reached for her wineglass, and took a sip, unnerved to see how unsteady her hand was. "Okay, this place is far too expensive, and this wine costs a fortune."

"You get what you pay for," he murmured with narrowed eyes.

"I know, I know," she said.

"Your Ryan doesn't take you to places like this?"

"Yes, of course, but—"

He cut off her words with his own. "I'm just a lowly security guard and my manners might not be up to par. And I definitely don't have the wherewithal to afford all of this. Is that it?"

"Yes. No, of course not, but—"

He held up one hand, palm out—the hand with his wedding band on it. "You're right. This is a bad idea," he said with thinly veiled anger.

The last thing she'd wanted to do was make him angry, or embarrass him, and she'd done both. He motioned to the waiter closest to them and asked for the bill.

"Rafe, no, I just—"

He drained the last of his wine, took the leather container with the bill and laid it by his glass. He stared at Megan while he took out his wallet, extracted a bill, then laid it on the leather holder. "Let's go," he muttered, and stood, not waiting to see if she followed.

She glanced at the money he'd left—a hundred dollar bill—then hurried after him. By the time she caught up, he was outside the front doors, waiting for the valet to get the car. She reached his side and looked up at him, but he was staring straight ahead. "Rafe, please, I was just trying to say that you didn't need to do this."

The SUV pulled up then. Rafe handed the valet a

tip, then got in. For a moment she was certain he was going to drive off before she could open the door. But she managed to get into the car before he put it in gear. The silence in the car was beyond painful, and she tried several times to think of something to say. Anything. She couldn't bear the wall between them. A wall she'd built by offending him, when she'd only been trying to protect him.

But she couldn't begin to find the words to apologize, so she sat back in the seat as they drove through the city. It took her a while to realize that Rafe wasn't taking her back to LynTech to get her car. He was taking her right home. "My car's at the office," she said, turning to him.

He kept going as if she hadn't said anything.

"Rafe, my car—"

"Is safe in the security garage," he muttered.

He wouldn't stay in the car with her any longer than necessary. "You've got your briefcase and your cell phone, don't you?"

"Of course."

He kept driving. "Then you can do your work at the loft."

"That isn't what I meant," she said. "I simply was pointing out that my car's not here and so I won't have a car to get to work tomorrow."

"Good point," he finally said.

But he didn't turn around. He kept going. "Rafe…" she said, frustration rising in her.

"Oh, come on," he finally muttered as they approached the street where the loft was. "People like you can call a taxi. You don't have to worry about money.''

"Stop it," she muttered.

He did stop, but not his words. Rather, the SUV at the curb in front of the loft. "Hell, I'll pay for a cab," he said. He braked with a lurch, then got out and opened her door. Before she could do anything he was pushing money at her. "Here, use what's left over for a tip."

She looked down at the bill in her hand. Another hundred dollars. "No," she gasped, and thrust his hand away.

They faced each other on the sidewalk for an interminable moment, then he slowly and deliberately folded the bill in quarters and tucked the bill into her blouse pocket with her cell phone.

"Keep it," he said, and went around to get in the car, leaving her standing there to watch him take off in a squeal of tires.

Chapter Twelve

Megan felt her legs go rubbery and tears burn her eyes as she hurried to the entrance of the loft. She fumbled in her briefcase to get her keys, and wanted to scream when they weren't there. "Think, think," she muttered to herself, more than aware of the deserted street and her vulnerability standing outside. "Think!" The keys. She'd had them in Mary's office, on top of her briefcase, and remembered picking them up when she went upstairs.

She'd gone into her cubicle, sorted the papers for Mr. Lawrence, and remembered having them in her hand in his office. Then… Her heart sank. She'd left them on Mr. Lawrence's desk. She could almost visualize them sitting by her briefcase when she'd put his envelope on the desk. And then Rafe had shown up, and she'd never thought about the keys again.

"Oh, damn," she breathed, looking around, without any idea what to do. Trig was long gone, and he hadn't given her the extra key or told her if it was hidden anywhere. And she didn't know anyone else in the warehouse. She looked at the call box and saw two

names by the lower loft addresses. M. Bordeaux and
R. E. Randall. She took a breath, then hit the buzzer
for M. Bordeaux, but it went unanswered. "Not
home," she muttered, and hit the other button. After
two buzzes, a voice came over the speaker. "Yes?"

"I'm sorry. I live upstairs and I locked myself out.
Could you buzz me in?"

"What's the name?"

"Gallagher."

"Nope, don't know any Gallagher living here," the
voice said, and she could tell it was male and older.

"Sir, I'm just staying here for a month, and I—"

"Nope, I'm not stupid. I know the scams out there
to get into buildings. You just go away," the voice
said, then cut off.

Megan stared at the call box, then reached in her
shirt for her phone. She watched it fade and die. She
hadn't charged it today, and the thing was dead and
useless.

"Great, just great," she muttered. "What a mess!"

"What's a mess?" a voice asked from behind her,
a voice that startled her so much that the briefcase fell
from her hold and landed on the ground at her feet.

She turned, and Rafe was there, hunkered down,
putting the things that had spilled on the ground back
into her briefcase. She stared at the top of his head,
totally unable to think of one thing to say while she
dealt with the overwhelming joy at seeing him there.
But the joy was short-lived when he stood with her
briefcase in his hands, and the dark eyes weren't filled
with any pleasure at all.

"Here," he said.

She took the case, hugging it to her chest. "What are you doing back here?" she asked.

"Why are you still outside?"

"I forgot my keys again. Now why are you here?"

"I forgot something," he said.

She put the phone back in her pocket and at the same time took out the folded currency. "Here."

He looked at the bill, but didn't move to take it. "I don't want that."

She balled it up in her hand. "Then what do you want?"

"How are you going to get inside?"

"I don't know. I guess I'll find a pay phone, get a cab and go back to work and try to find my keys."

"Your cell phone?"

"Dead."

"Sad," he said with a shake of his head. "Why don't you just ring someone in the building to let you inside?"

"I already did, and the only one to answer thought I was trying to get into the building to rob him or something." She shrugged. "Besides, even if I get in, I can't open the door to the loft."

Rafe looked up and down the street, then back at her. "How's the cat getting in and out these days?"

"Through the transom over the fire escape window."

"The transom's open?"

"It was when I left."

"Stay right here. I'll see what I can do," he said, then jogged off to the far side of the warehouse, to a narrow walkway that led to the alley behind the struc-

ture. He disappeared from sight, but she could hear his
shoes striking the ground until they faded off into the
distance. And she was alone.

She hugged her briefcase to her, and that sense of
loneliness started to seep back into her spirit. But before long, the door buzzed and clicked. Grateful to
finally be inside, she practically ran to the elevator and
headed upstairs. When she reached the loft, Rafe stood
in the doorway.

"What did you do?" she asked.

"It's a long story," he said, brushing his hands together. "But I got in."

She fought the urge to brush at the soot on his
cheek. She put her briefcase on a table by the entry,
closed the door and turned to see Rafe disappearing
into the kitchen. Then there was the sound of water
running. "Just cleaning up," he called out to her.

"Sure," she murmured, and kicked off her shoes.
Then he was there, coming back into the room, his
shirt untucked from his slacks and completely unbuttoned. The soot was gone from his face and hands, but
his shirt was ruined. "I owe you a shirt," she said as
he came closer to where she stood.

He shrugged. "Don't worry about it."

"Are you going to tell me how you got in?"

He motioned to the fire escape window and she noticed it was half-open now. "The transom was open,
and I managed to get the lock off the window. The
rest, as they say, was a piece of cake."

"But how did you get up on the fire escape to begin
with?"

He looked a bit sheepish. "Old habits die hard, I'm afraid."

"What does that mean?"

"When I was a kid, we played a game to see who could get a fire escape ladder down the fastest. I usually won." He raked both hands through his slightly damp hair and gave her a wry grin. "No, I wasn't poor and roaming the streets looking for houses to rob. I just had a knack for getting into places. Fire escapes are easy, except pretty dirty." He brushed at his shirt, and it opened slightly, exposing more of his sleek chest. "Back then I didn't care about the mess."

Megan's mouth was suddenly dry, and she averted her eyes from his naked chest, back up to his face, but not fast enough to stop him from realizing where her thoughts were going. The smile changed to something more…what? Satisfied? That didn't make sense. "I'll…I'll get you another shirt," she said, her voice tight as he came closer, stopping about a foot away from her.

"No. Thanks, but no," he murmured softly.

She crossed her arms on her chest, as if that could protect her from what was happening. "You never said why you came back," she managed to murmur, barely recognizing her own voice.

Rafe knew exactly why he'd come back to this woman. He'd known the minute he'd pulled away from the curb that he had to return. But once he'd seen her, he'd withdrawn from the truth. Now it stared him right in the eye. He'd come back because he had to. He couldn't just drive away. He had to be here, and do what he'd wanted to for what seemed forever.

He touched her shoulders, felt her tense at the contact, then leaned even closer and found her lips with his.

As soon as he tasted her and felt her body pressing against his, he knew that he'd done the right thing. The only thing possible. And when her mouth opened for him, and her hands tentatively slipped around his waist, under his shirt, he was sure he was where he should be. He shuddered when her hands skimmed up his naked back, then his shirt was being pushed off his shoulders, and fell to the floor at his feet.

When her hands touched him, Rafe came alive, and when he breathed in her essence, that feeling grew. He felt a sense of homecoming, of need and desire all focusing on one person, and it was as if he'd been given a gift. A wonderful gift. A gift that could literally save his life. He drank her in, finding the front of her shirt, getting the buttons undone, then pushing aside the silky material. He heard something thud on the floor, probably her phone, but he didn't care. He dipped his head to her throat, tasting the soft heat near her ear, then lower, to the pulse that beat wildly there.

Her arms were around his neck, her body arching to his, and the lace of her bra was all that was between them. And that was gone quickly. Then her naked breasts were crushed against his chest, and he could literally feel her heart beating against his. And that life seemed to be everywhere. It was intense and sweet, and achingly beautiful, filling his soul and righting his world.

He wanted her. He needed her. All of her. He shifted, scooping her up in his arms, feeling her cling to him, her face turned into his chest and her lips tasting his skin. He carried her to the bedroom, into soft shadows barely touched by filtered moonlight from the high windows, and crossed to the bed. After lowering her onto the linens, he stood back, looking down at her, and the wonder of her beauty flooded through him.

Her hair was loose, her blouse and bra gone. Her breasts were high and perfect, with dusky pink nipples hard with desire. Her eyes were on him, her breath rapid and shallow, and he couldn't move. He felt uncertain, as if this was his first time. Rafe needed her with a passion that threatened to consume him, but he was unwilling to take her if she wasn't ready. And he knew once he touched her again he wouldn't be able to stop.

Her hands lifted toward him, and she shifted, moving closer. "Rafe?" she whispered.

He stood motionless. "Are you sure?" he heard himself ask.

"Love me," she breathed. "Please."

He moved then, going to her, and he'd been right. There was no stopping now. No hope of ever walking away from her. Her arms were around him, and he found the waistband of her slacks, managed to undo it and push them down. She lifted her hips, her hands fumbling with the material, too, before she kicked them off. Then her panties were gone, and he laid his hand flat on her taut stomach.

He felt her shudder softly, and as his hands went lower, she lifted her hips to him and he found her center. She moaned, the sound mingling with his low exhalation of air. The feel of her was overwhelming, the heat and moisture inviting and driving him. He moved back enough to get his own pants off, and she helped, unzipping the fly, freeing him from the confines of the heavy material. Before he got free of the slacks, her hands were at his waist, tugging on his briefs, pulling them down. Then she touched him.

He groaned, shaking from the intensity of the feeling of her hand around him. That was enough. Enough. He moved, shifting over her, bracing himself with his hands on either side of her shoulders, looking down at her, loving her. That thought came and stayed. *Loving her.* Loving Megan. He let it stay while he felt her, tested her with his strength. When she lifted to him, he slipped into her. *Loving Megan.* He moved slowly, filling her, easing as far as he could into her. Her legs came up, around his hips, holding him there for what seemed an eternity of pleasure, then he started to move.

She went with him, the motions slow at first, almost hesitant, but as the sensations grew, they speeded up, faster and faster. Higher and higher. *Loving Megan,* he thought again in that last moment before he found a center to his universe, one that was new and wonderful. He knew that she was his future, his hope and his love. His voice mingled with hers when he cried out, ripples of completion running through him. Then slowly, ever so slowly, he sank back, sated.

He stayed with her as long as he could, then they rolled onto their sides, facing each other, her leg over his thigh, her hand against his heart and his arm on her waist. She kissed his chest, snuggled into him and sighed deeply. He thought she whispered, "Thank you," but couldn't be sure.

He held her against him, kissing the top of her head, feeling her heat along his body and letting one fact settle into him: he loved her.

MEGAN STIRRED, then felt Rafe against her side, his arm around her and his hand resting just above her left breast. She stayed very still in the shadows of the loft and let the feeling of belonging seep into her. Belonging. Right here. With Rafe. And as that settled into her soul, so did the fact that she was in love with the man holding her. She took a shuddering breath.

"You're awake?" Rafe whispered, and she felt his lips press against her forehead.

She shifted closer to him, holding him tightly. "Yes."

"Good," he breathed, and turned more toward her, his hand finding her left breast, cupping its weight. "Very good."

She loved him. The thought transformed everything. His touch, his breath on her skin, his body against hers. It was a monumental realization that she now knew had been there from almost the first moment they'd spoken. But it had taken her all this time to figure it out.

She pressed a kiss to his naked chest, relishing the damp saltiness on her lips, then found his nipple with her tongue, and felt him shudder. Oh, she loved him. She really loved him, and when he drew her closer, his hands roaming over her nakedness as if he'd known her forever, she went to him. She went with joy and wonder, and a sense of finally finding her place in the world.

She thought about nothing but being with him as she rolled toward him. He lifted her and his hands spanned her waist, brought her on top of him. Then slowly, very slowly, he entered her fully. There was a long moment when neither of them stirred, when the sensations threatened to consume her. Then she moved, her hair falling forward as she touched her lips to his, and she began to rock.

She gasped at the first thrust, the second, the third. Then everything speeded up. Faster and faster they moved, her need for completion, overwhelming. She felt his hands at her back, then on her bottom, pulling her forward, sending him deeper into her. The feelings went past reason, almost more than she could bear, then she arched back and heard a voice cry out. Her voice. Rafe was deep within her, their connection perfect, and she let the wonder stream through her.

Ecstasy filled her, consumed her for a long, endless time. Then she felt herself coming back to reality. The reality of being with Rafe, of being one with another person in a way she'd never known existed until that moment in time. She rested on his chest, his hands tangled in her hair, and she heard the echo of his ragged breaths against her face, mingled with the wild thudding of his heart.

They lay together until their heartbeats slowed, and then she rolled to one side, hating to break the contact, then sighing as Rafe gathered her into his arms, holding her tightly against him. She closed her eyes, content in a way that seemed almost unreal to her. Content. Belonging. Here. She sighed heavily and fell asleep with Rafe's heart beating against her cheek.

Rafe felt Megan fall asleep, but he was wide awake. He stared into the shadows over them, waiting for that moment when he knew he'd betrayed everything he'd had in his life. That moment when he knew this was wrong. But it never came. There was no sense that he'd been unfaithful to the memory of his wife. He'd loved Gabriella, but in a stunning moment of truth, he knew it was okay to love Megan. This love was all hers. It wasn't some secondhand version. It was different and unique, all Megan, and it filled his heart.

He felt his eyes smart as relief flowed over him. It was okay. Okay! He loved her. He kissed the top of her head, inhaling that scent of flowers and sweetness that clung to her. He loved her, and it was okay. He closed his eyes, a sense of completion filling him, as if he'd found what he'd been looking for. That didn't make sense, but he wasn't going down that road now. Not yet.

There was a muffled ringing sound. A phone. His cell phone? He eased away from Megan, freeing his hand and reaching toward the floor for it. Finally propped up on one elbow, he said in a low voice, "Yes?"

"You told me to call if there was activity from LynTech after eight."

It took Rafe a long moment to recognize the voice of one of the people he'd contacted over the weekend when he'd been in Fort Worth having Greg checked by their family doctor. Stanley Green was one of the best wiretappers in the business. "What have you got?"

"Out line use from an office marked on the grid as empty."

"What use?"

"Computer fax."

"Any destination?" he asked just above a whisper as he pushed himself up and sat on the edge of the bed. He listened and then replied, "Yeah, just where I thought it would go."

A few days ago he'd finally realized what was probably going on and had set things up with Stanley. But he hadn't expected results this quickly. "Good. Get that to me at..." He looked over at Megan, snuggled into the mussed linen. "Send it to my house. I'll look at it and get back to you in two hours."

"You got it," Stanley said, and hung up.

Rafe flipped his phone shut, then turned on the bed. A sliver of moonlight had invaded the room and washed over Megan. He felt a response deep inside him, but fought it. He couldn't stay. He had to get to the house, though the thought of leaving her made him ache. He leaned over her, brushing his lips across the silkiness of her naked shoulder. She trembled slightly, sighed and resettled into sleep.

He eased off the bed, found his clothes and dressed quickly, though the soiled shirt was really rumpled now. As he pushed the phone back in his pocket, he went around the bed and looked down at Megan one last time. *Enough,* he told himself as his eyes skimmed over her—the curve of her shoulder, her naked breasts, the flare of her hip. Enough for now. But he knew he'd never get enough of her.

He reached for the sheet and tugged it over her nakedness, then stood back and looked at the wedding band on his finger. Slowly, he slipped it off and put it in his pocket. He'd find a safe place to keep it, but he wouldn't wear it anymore.

Rafe walked out of the bedroom, crossed to the workstation and turned on a small side light. Quickly, he found a sheet of paper and a pen, scrawled, "Sorry, have to leave. Talk later," then hesitated before signing it, "Rafe." It wasn't what he wanted to write, but that would come later, when he saw her again, and they could talk face-to-face. He found some tape and fastened the note on the inside of the front door.

He left the loft, hurrying down to the street and his car. He got in, took out his cell phone and put in a call to Zane. Tomorrow he'd see Megan. That simple thought brought him real pleasure. Tomorrow. And for the first time in a long time, he looked forward to all the tomorrows in his life.

Megan awoke alone at dawn. "Rafe?" she called. There was no answer. She saw the cat on top of the wall, but she couldn't hear anyone else in the loft. She got up, padded naked into the main room, then spotted the note on the door. "Sorry, had to leave." She hadn't heard him leave. "Talk later." Yes, they'd talk later, but first she had something she had to do. She went back into the bedroom, passing the rumpled bed, and went into the bathroom.

Her shower that morning was long, the fantasies very real and breathtaking. And she let them come.

She relished them. The idea of Rafe there with her, his hands on her, his skin slippery... When she finally got out and dried off, she dressed in taupe linen slacks and a rich gold shirt. When she stepped back out into the main room, she stopped when the phone rang. She hurried to it, wanting it to be Rafe, but felt her heart lurch when Ryan spoke over the line.

"Megan?"

She glanced at the clock by the computer. It was five in the morning in California. "Ryan. It's so early," she said, because she really didn't know what else to say.

"I've been giving you space. I wanted you to think on what you said about breaking things off. I wanted..." His voice trailed off, then he said, "Is it really over?"

Megan closed her eyes. "Yes. I'm sorry, I can't do this. I told you. It's not right. I'll send your grand-mother's ring back as soon as I can. I love you, but I'm not in love with you."

"Are you sure?"

She was so very sure. She loved Rafe. Now she knew what love was supposed to be. And she knew how much it could hurt, too. "I'm sure."

There was silence, then the line clicked on the other end, and Ryan was gone. She took a deep breath, and knew she'd let go of Ryan and any plans they had the moment she'd met Rafe.

Chapter Thirteen

For the rest of the day, Megan didn't see Rafe. She went to LynTech and was sent down to the center to work on tax forms for the money made at the ball. She waited, expecting Rafe to come into Mary's office at any moment, but time moved with aching slowness, and he didn't appear. Around noon, Mary came in and said, "How's it going?"

"Almost done." She sat back in the chair and stretched her arms to ease the tension in her shoulders. "Are Greg and Gabe in today?"

"Yes, they are, and Greg is doing fine," Mary said, crossing to the desk to pick up her purse. "Now, I need to leave for a little while." She glanced at the wall clock. "I'll be back around one."

Megan had tried to sound casual asking about the boys, and really tried to ask the next question in a casual manner. "Who brought the boys in?"

Mary looked up at her. "Oh, their baby-sitter."

"Not Rafe...Mr. Diaz?"

"No, he wasn't here. He probably had to get right

to work.'' Mary started for the door. ''See you soon,'' she said, and left.

Megan sat there for a while, then decided to do what she wanted to do instead of acting mature and controlled. She went out into the main room, where she spotted the twins. They were huddled over something on the floor, both of them intent on the object of their fascination. She went closer, trying to absorb the fact that she was so happy to see the two of them. Then Gabe turned, as if he sensed her there, and smiled, the smile that exposed the dimple...just like his dad's.

In a blur, Gabe was on his feet and he ran right at her, but this time she welcomed the contact, and the feeling of his tiny arms hugging her around her knees. ''Megan!''

She crouched near him, ruffling his dark hair. ''Hey, buddy boy, how are you doing?''

''We rode horses and did stuff, and had a good time,'' Gabe said. Then Greg stood up, hesitated, then came over to look up at her.

''Yeah, we did cowboy stuff and I didn't fall.'' He had a small Band-Aid on his forehead, but he looked as if he'd had a great victory. ''I was real careful and I never fell.''

''Wow, that's great,'' she said, wondering where on earth Rafe had taken them to do all of this. ''I don't know if I could stay on a horse without falling.''

Greg came closer. ''When we go next time to Mamaw's, you come, too, and you can ride.''

''Yeah.'' Gabe touched her shoulder. ''I won't let you fall.''

Megan's eyes burned suddenly, and she instinctively hugged both boys to her. She loved their dad, and shockingly, she knew she loved them, too. It didn't make sense, not when she'd spent most of her life convinced that she didn't even like kids that much.

She must have let the hug last too long, because both boys started to squirm and she reluctantly let them go. She blinked rapidly, then said, "So, what are you two doing over here?"

Gabe looked bashful, and Greg shrugged. "Nothin'."

"Really?"

"Huh, nothin'," Gabe echoed, moving to block her view.

She stood and looked behind them. The rat. "Charlie, huh?"

"Yeah," Gabe whispered. "Don't get scared or nothing. He's just hungry, and we're going to feed him."

She smiled down at them. "Don't worry, I won't get scared. He's in his cage and you two know how to handle him."

"Daddy said we shouldn't never do that again with Charlie."

Daddy. "I'll thank him when I see him," she murmured.

"He's working," Greg said. "He's real busy today."

So he was here. "You go ahead and take care of Charlie."

The boys went back to the rat, and she looked around the center, fighting the urge to head out and find Rafe.

But she waited as long as she could and then knew she couldn't wait until six when he picked up the boys. She needed to see him, alone. She left the office, skirting the kids on her way through the play area. Gabe spotted her and waved. She waved back and smiled, then left to find Rafe.

Ten minutes later, Megan was no closer to finding him than when she'd started. That was when she spotted the other guard, Brad, by the elevators, hitting the Up button. "Excuse me?" she called to him.

He turned, saw her, then smiled and tapped the bill of his cap. "Yes, ma'am. What can I do for you?"

"I was looking for Rafe Diaz, one of the guards?"

"Oh, sure," he said, his smile shifting as his eyes flicked over her. "Sure."

He was making her uncomfortable, but she tried to be polite. "Do you know where he is?"

"On rounds. Could be anywhere. I can call him on the radio if it's an emergency?"

It was an emergency, but not one he'd consider critical. "Oh, no, it's not. I'll just wait until later."

"Yes, ma'am," he said as the elevator dinged softly and the doors opened. "Going up?" he asked.

There was no way she was going to get into the elevator with this man. "No, I'm not," she said, and turned to head down the hallway. She didn't look back, but went to the stairwell door and stepped inside, then headed up.

She got to the second-floor door, started to push it open, but stopped when she heard a familiar voice: Rafe's. "What are you talking about?" he asked. He was here, and she almost stepped out into the corridor, but stopped dead when someone else spoke.

"Yeah, she's hunting for you, looking kind of panicky, actually. I told her I'd call you on the radio, but she passed." Megan peeked out just far enough to see Rafe in his uniform, and all she could see of Brad were his hands gesticulating as he spoke. "Yeah, she's got it good for you, guy."

Megan flushed at his words. Was she that transparent? Even to someone like Brad? "Well, I'll check on her later," Rafe said.

He started to turn in her direction, but Brad grabbed his upper arm. Rafe turned, pulling back from the contact. "Hey, I owe you, buddy," Brad said.

"No, no, you don't," Rafe said.

"Oh, but I do." The hand went out of sight, then reappeared in her line of vision, holding money. "Here's twenty. I'll get the rest to you on payday."

"No," Rafe said, not taking it.

"Yeah, I make good on my bets. Don't bet unless you can afford to lose, I always say, although I thought I had a sure bet. I didn't think you had it in you to get her to melt down, but damn, you got her more then melted." He laughed, an ugly sound that seemed to echo in the stairwell. "She's crazy for you. I can tell. Imagine, someone like her with someone like one of us. Who would have thought?"

A bet? It had all been a bet? Megan felt as if a fist had been driven into her stomach.

"Hey, forget about it," Rafe said. There was no outrage, no denial. "Keep your money."

Brad stuffed the bills into Rafe's breast pocket,

much the way Rafe had pushed the hundred-dollar bill into hers. "No way, man. Good job. You've made me proud. Just knowing you got her, someone as snobby as she is, as cold and uppity... Damn, you're good."

Megan backed up blindly, letting the door click shut. And if the railing hadn't been there, she would have gone tumbling down the stairs. It was all a bet? The ache in her middle made her nauseous. A bet. He'd done it to prove he could? Nothing he'd said or done was real. Nothing. She blindly reached for the railing, and somehow made it down to the ground floor.

When she touched the door, she couldn't open it. She leaned back against the cold walls and slowly sank down until she was crouched, her arms around her legs, her forehead pressed to her knees. And Megan Gallagher cried as if her heart would break. But in fact, it was already broken.

RAFE GOT RID OF BRAD as quickly as he could, then went to call Zane. He knew what was going on now, and he needed Zane there when he took action. They agreed to meet in Zane's private offices in an hour. Rafe knew what he'd do with that hour. Brad, as disgusting as the encounter with him had been, had only reminded him how much he needed to see Megan. With everything in place now, he had time. He had an hour, and he was going to take it.

He'd tried to go and see her today at the center, but hadn't been able to get down there until now. He rode down in the elevator, got out at the main floor and crossed to the brightly colored doors. He'd see her, talk a bit, then make a date for tonight, when he would tell her the truth—about who he was, and that no matter what his name was, or what he did for a living, he loved her.

He went inside the center, thankful that the kids were napping and all was quiet. He nodded to the teenager sitting with the sleeping children, then went past them all, past the cartoon tree, into the back hall to the office.

He approached the open door, stopping before going inside when he saw Megan at the desk. Rafe felt like a teenager with a crush, the way his heart raced at the sight of her bent over an open ledger. Quietly he went inside, needing to touch her, but not daring to just yet. ''Megan?'' he said softly, and her head snapped up.

Her blue eyes were on him, but there was no warmth in them. They looked almost afraid, then they narrowed and she sat back. ''Rafe,'' she said.

He felt awkward and didn't know where to start. ''We need to talk.'' That sounded reasonable.

''Talk?'' she asked, sitting back in her chair. ''No, we don't, and I've got work to do.'' With that she stood and came around the desk, as if she was leaving. He stopped her by taking her upper arm. He was struck at how delicate she felt in his grasp and how badly he wanted to hold on to her. He drew back and she turned, looking up at him, her eyes softly blurred as if she'd been crying.

''We have to talk…about last night.''

''What about it?'' she asked in a low voice.

This couldn't be happening. ''Last night…'' Then he thought he understood. ''I was going to wake you when I left, but there was an emergency, and I left the note.''

"No problem," she murmured tightly.

"Megan, for God's sake, what's wrong?"

"Nothing. Last night was last night. This is now." She crossed her arms on her breasts and didn't blink. "What difference does any of it make?" She looked pale and her expression was pinched at the mouth. "It was nothing. Just a…" She shrugged, gave a vague, fluttery gesture with one hand. "Nothing."

Frustration and pain drove him to take her by her shoulders, but she didn't fight him. She didn't scream or push him away. She just stood there, looking right at him, her expression bleak. "Nothing?" he breathed.

"Nothing," she echoed.

Then he finally understood, and bitterness rose harshly in his throat. "Oh, sure," he said, and let her go. He could barely stand to look at her as the realization sunk in. "I understand. I should have understood long before last night, but…" He pushed his hands in his pockets as an ache formed in his middle, and he had to force himself not to hunch protectively. What a fool he'd been, misreading everything because he was so needy.

"But what?" she breathed.

"I thought you were different. That you had a heart, a soul." He shook his head. "My mistake."

"I guess we both misread the situation," she said. "But thank goodness we didn't get too involved."

She could speak for herself on that one. The last time he'd felt pain like this, he'd been grieving. Now it was mingled with anger and disgust and a sense of complete loss. "Yeah, thank goodness. Who needs a cold, manipulative, self-serving—"

She stared at him, her eyes overly bright, then she hit him. Her hand struck his face, and he didn't move. Fire radiated in his cheek, but he didn't touch it. She pulled her hand back, staring at it in horror, as if it had functioned on its own. Then her cell phone rang, and they both froze, waiting to see what she would do.

She didn't answer it. Instead, she turned from him and left the room.

She was gone and he was alone. He sank down on the pink plastic chair, buried his head in his hands and tried to blot out everything. But nothing stopped the pain radiating through him, or the way he'd let himself care so much. He wouldn't make that mistake again. Ever.

MEGAN DIDN'T THINK anything could hurt worse than when she'd heard Rafe talking to Brad. She'd been wrong. Seeing him that last time had been worse. She worked the rest of the day on the nineteenth floor, and by the time she went back down to the center at five-thirty, she'd spent most of the afternoon in the ladies' room near Legal, crying. She'd given up trying to breathe correctly, or thinking she could concentrate on anything. She was leaving.

All she had to do was pick up the paperwork she'd left in Mary's office, then she was gone. She'd leave it on Mr. Lawrence's desk, then head to the loft. From there, she was going back to San Francisco. She'd pack, make sure the cat had food, then get on a plane and go home. Simple. Just do it.

She went into the center, skirting around the few kids watching a video on TV, but never made it out before Gabe spotted her. He scrambled to his feet and ran toward her, tangling his arms around her legs and smiling up at her with that dimple. She swallowed hard and crouched in front of him as Greg ran over in turn.

"We want to go riding horses, and Mary says we can't," Greg said. "You talk to her. You tell her we ride all the time."

"Sweetheart, I can't tell her anything. It's up to your daddy to talk to her about things like that."

Gabe moved closer and put his arm around Megan's neck. The action only made her pain more unbearable. She had to leave their dad, and now them. The fact was she loved all of them, no matter what, but she couldn't be here. "You talk to Daddy," Gabe said.

She closed her eyes. "Honey, you have to do that."

"Oh, okay," Gabe sighed. "But he's real busy. *Real* busy," he said with emphasis and a roll of his huge dark eyes. "He's always real busy."

"Well, I'm busy right now, too." She took a breath. "But I just wanted to say that I'm sure happy we met."

"Me, too," Greg said.

"Yeah, me, too," Gabe echoed.

She stood, her legs shaky, and tried to smile at them. "You two go and watch the movie. I've got to get some things from the office."

Greg ran off, but Gabe hesitated for a minute. "You sad, Megan?" he asked, studying her intently.

"Me, sad?" she asked. "No, I'm not sad."

"Good," he said, relieved, then ran off after his brother.

She turned from them, moving quickly toward the office, and thankfully got inside before the burning in her eyes turned to tears. She hadn't cried much in her life, but hadn't been able to stop for most of the afternoon. She crossed to the pink chair and dropped down in it, sorting through the stuff on the desk to find the ever-present box of Kleenex.

She tugged some tissues out of the box and dabbed at her eyes, then blew her nose. She never heard the door open, and didn't realize someone was there until she heard Mary say, "Megan, honey, are you all right?"

She could have made up some lies about allergies or something, but didn't have it in her at that moment. She sagged back into the chair and looked up at her friend. "I'm leaving. I'm going back to San Francisco."

The woman came closer. "Oh, no. That Mr. Lawrence didn't fire you, did he?"

A few weeks ago that would have been the worst thing Megan could imagine happening, but not now. "No, he didn't." She still had to tell her boss. "I just have to get back to the city." She wiped at her eyes again and balled the Kleenex in her right hand. "Don't worry about this job, though. I have the center's business all worked out, and the incorporation papers are ready to file. Anyone can finish it for you."

"I don't care about that," Mary said quickly. "I mean, I do, but if this isn't about work, what is it about?"

Megan had never been one to confide in anyone about her feelings or her fears, but for some reason, when Mary touched her clenched hand and sat on the edge of the desk, she found herself spilling everything to the woman. She told her things she'd only thought about to herself, things that she wouldn't have dreamt of telling another living person. And once she started, she couldn't stop.

"And he had a lousy bet. A bet!" she finally declared, finishing with a choking gasp.

The room was silent, then Mary moved around behind the desk, sat down in the wooden chair and faced Megan. She leaned forward and took both of Megan's hands in hers. The tears were quietly falling now, and they wouldn't stop.

"Okay, you think he did all of this for a bet?"

She pulled her hands back and hugged her arms around herself. "I know he did. I heard him." She reached for another Kleenex and wiped at her eyes. "He called me the 'ice princess' and took money from that man." She bit her lip hard. "Twenty dollars, and he owed him more."

Mary sat back and sighed. "What a mess. But you know..." Her voice trailed off and she sat looking down at her hands in her lap.

"What?" Megan finally asked.

Mary looked at her, her pale eyes behind her glasses dead serious. "I shouldn't intrude on this. I mean, you're sure what you heard, and what you have to do, but…''

Megan felt her nerves fraying even more. "But what?" she finally asked as she shredded the Kleenex in her hands.

"Before you heard this conversation, what did you think of Rafe?"

She shrugged. "I thought…" She exhaled and spoke in a rush. "I thought I loved him and that he was…he was the one." She held up her left hand, with its bare ring finger. "I broke up with Ryan, everything, because of Rafe."

"Even though he's just a security guard, you love him?"

Megan sighed harshly. "That never mattered. He's who he is, but I thought he was someone he's not."

"But what if he is who you think he is? What if he's everything and more than that?"

"But he's not."

"Indulge me on this."

"Okay," she whispered, tossing the Kleenex onto the desk and clasping her hands tightly in front of her. "Okay."

"What if he's everything you thought he was, and you walk away? What if he might be the love of your life and you never tell him? What if you go through life without him, and what if, somewhere down the road, you find out you were wrong, very wrong? Oh, you might have a good life, but not with him. What then?"

Megan hadn't thought any further ahead than her plane flight. "What if he's not what I thought at all?

What if I'm right about him using me?'' Even saying the words hurt. ''What if that's true?''

''It very well could be,'' Mary said softly. ''But it might not be, too.'' She leaned forward again and covered Megan's hands with hers one more time. ''Honey, don't ever live your life with regrets. Don't walk away before you know for absolutely certain it's the right thing to do.'' She tightened her hold. ''Listen to me, and listen good. I did walk away years ago, from someone. I loved another man and I had a good life. A good life. But I didn't have the life I would have had if I'd only tried one more time to understand what was going on.''

Megan blinked rapidly, her lashes damp with tears. ''Who..?'' And she knew. ''You and Mr. Lewis,'' she said, and it wasn't a question.

Mary actually flushed slightly and drew back after patting Megan's hands. ''Was it that obvious?'' she murmured.

''No, not at all, but…'' Megan remembered seeing them together in this office. ''I thought you were good friends. I didn't know….''

''Well, years ago I left Robert when things looked pretty bad. I went on, married my husband and had a good life. But I never forgot Robert. And when we met again, I found out that all I would have had to do was talk to him honestly. He thought I didn't love him, and he walked away when I did. And it was a total waste. Don't make my mistake, Megan. Don't give up until you know for sure there's nothing there.''

Megan gazed at her wordlessly.

"Would it be any worse if you found out you were right?" Mary asked softly.

She shook her head. "No, it couldn't be."

"Then find out, honey, before you do anything else." The phone rang but Mary ignored it. "Please, just find out."

Megan swallowed hard and swiped at her eyes. Mary was right. She couldn't feel worse, and she really needed to know everything. "Okay, I'll try to talk to him."

"That's wonderful," Mary said. "No matter how it turns out, you won't regret it."

Megan just hoped that was true. "I'll try to find him before I leave."

"He'll be here at six for the boys. Although maybe you'd rather meet him alone?"

She wasn't sure she could be alone with him and do anything rational. "I'll...I'll find him," she said as the phone started to ring again. "The phone?"

Mary patted her hand, then stood and reached for the receiver. "Yes?" She was silent for a moment, then said, "I'll be right there." She hung up and looked at Megan. "I need to get upstairs. A problem." She looked flustered. "I'll talk to you later," she said, and hurried off.

Megan put all of her papers together in her briefcase, then left the office. When she stepped out into the play area, the boys were there with the teenager, watching a video about a mermaid. They both turned when she got close, and both scrambled to their feet to hurry over to her. They were jumping up and down, babbling about horses and cowboys and animals and ranches. None of it made sense to her, but distracted as she felt today, she wasn't listening too carefully.

"Miss Gallagher?" The teenager was coming toward her. "Do you know where Mrs. Garner went?"

"She had something she had to do upstairs."

"Did she say how long she'd be gone?"

"No, she didn't."

The girl frowned, glancing at the oversize watch on her thin wrist. "She knows I have to leave now. I'm going to be late for tryouts. They're doing a play at the community center near where I live and I'm up for a part." She nibbled on her lip. "I hate to be late."

Megan patted both boys on the head as they clung to her legs. "Is it just Greg and Gabe left?"

"Yeah, their dad's coming in a few minutes. Do you think you could sit with them until he got here?"

"Oh, I don't know, I—"

"Please, they're crazy about you. They talk about you all the time, and about Charlie scaring you, and things."

"Please stay," the twins were saying as they jumped up and down. "Please, Megan, please."

She looked down at them and found herself agreeing. "Okay, go on to your rehearsal," she told the girl.

"I owe you," she said, and ran off toward the back of the center.

Megan looked down at the two upturned faces and wondered when she'd changed so drastically. They were wonderful kids. And if everything with Rafe turned out to be as she thought it was, it would only add to her pain to walk away from the boys, too. She'd have to, but she wasn't sure how she could do that and survive.

Chapter Fourteen

"How about reading a book?" she asked, remembering what Quint had told her. *When in doubt, find a book with an animal in it and read it to them.* She'd have a few minutes with them, and she suddenly wanted that very much.

"Yeah, sure," Greg said, grabbing her hand and trying to drag her to the bookshelves beyond the tree. She went with the two of them, and Greg found a huge book with a horse on the cover. They settled in the corner on the carpet, and with a boy on each side, she started to read the story of a pony who dreamt of being a racehorse.

She read the story twice, and was being begged to read it again when she glanced at the wall clock and saw it was ten minutes after six. Rafe was late, and a part of her was relieved to have had a bit more time before her life changed forever. She started the book again, and the boys were as rapt as the first time. When she finished and closed it, she glanced nervously at the clock once more. Twenty minutes after six.

She put the book away, then got to her feet and held

out her hands to the boys. "Your dad's late. Why don't we go and see if we can find him?"

"Yeah," Greg said, grabbing her hand, while Gabe took the other.

The three of them left the center, going out into the main reception area, but there was no sign of Rafe, or any security guard by the doors. That was unusual. "How about going up in the elevator?" she asked the boys.

"Way up?" Greg asked with real anticipation in his face.

"Well, a few floors up," she said, and crossed to the elevators. She let Gabe push the button, and when the doors opened, they got in. The boys never let go of her as they turned to face the closing doors. Greg pushed the button for the level Security was on, and they started up.

They checked the Security offices, but no one was there, and Megan decided to go up to her own floor. Rafe had been there a few nights around this time. *I was looking for you...* She tried to get his words out of her mind and concentrate on the boys, who were enjoying the elevator ride. She didn't think Rafe would be looking for her now. The elevator stopped and the three of them stepped out into the reception area of Legal.

Ellen was at her desk, hurriedly stuffing things into her purse, and she looked up at Megan. "Hold the elevator!" she said, running around the desk and toward them. She got inside, and by the time Megan turned, the doors were closing and Ellen was gone.

Greg tugged hard on Megan's hand. "What's that smell?"

She took one whiff and knew what it was. Smoke. She looked around and saw a wispy cloud in the hallway that lead down to Mr. Lawrence's office. Then she heard voices, loud voices, one of them yelling "Get out of my way!" There was a sound of scuffling, then someone was coming right at them. Brad McMillan. Running hard. Megan saw Rafe right behind him. At first she thought they were running from the smoke, but Brad pushed past them, almost knocking them over in the process.

Then Rafe was there, his hat gone, his shirt half untucked, and he stopped when he saw her and the boys. "What are you doing up here?" he demanded, grabbing her by one arm. "Get them out of here! Now!"

The moment he spoke, a loud warning siren began to wail, and sprinklers came on overhead. Water was everywhere. "No elevator," Rafe said, and caught her arm, all but dragging her and the boys toward the stairwell. He pushed open the door, then pulled them with him. "Get down to the bottom level, and find Zane Holden. He should be back by now. Tell him McMillan's going to the roof."

She heard footsteps pounding on the metal stairs, but they were above her. She must have just been staring at Rafe, the way the boys were, because he suddenly cupped her face in both his hands. "Megan, go, now. Find Zane and tell him, but most importantly, you and the boys get out of here. Now. Get out of the building."

She wanted to say she wasn't going anywhere without him, but she could feel the boys shaking, and she knew she didn't have a choice. "Rafe, please, come with us."

He hesitated, and she knew he wanted to. Then he shook his head. "I'll be right behind you."

"Daddy?" Greg said asked, his voice quavering.

"You go with Megan and I'll be right down," he said, then he looked back at her. "Stay with my boys." He hesitated, then took off, heading up the stairs.

She knew in that moment that her heart was going with him, and that Mary had been right. Megan couldn't leave, not until she knew for sure what she had here, or what she didn't have. She turned with the boys and started down the stairs as fast as they could go.

Thankfully, they did what she said, and never faltered, finally reaching ground level. She pushed the fire door open and hurried into the hallway beyond where the air was still blessedly free of smoke. The three of them almost ran into firemen rushing toward the stairs.

"It's up on the nineteenth floor in Legal," she said to them. "A lot of smoke, and there are two men up there going toward the roof." The fire captain called out orders, told her to get outside, and his men followed him into the stairwell.

Megan backed up, holding tightly to both of the boys, then turned and almost ran into Zane Holden. The man was not in his usual suit, but in jeans and a chambray shirt, his hair mussed, with the shadow of a beard on his jaw. He saw the boys, then her. "Where is he?"

"Rafe, he…he said to tell you it's McMillan and he's after him."

The man blanched. "Where?"

"He was going after him to the roof."

"Oh, God," Zane said, then grabbed the arm of another firefighter. "There's two men on the roof, both in security guard uniforms. "Help Rafe, no matter what. Just make sure he gets down safely."

The man nodded, then went after the others.

Zane turned to Megan and, surprisingly, put his arm around her shoulders. She hadn't realized until then that she was shaking, too. "It's okay," he said, then let her go to crouch in front of the boys. "Your daddy's okay. He's really smart, and he'll be back down really soon."

"Sure," Greg said. "Daddy's real smart and brave."

"You bet he is," Zane said, then stood and faced Megan. "I think we met very briefly at the ball. In case you don't remember, I'm Zane Holden. I had no idea that you and Rafe…" He lead her away from the building. "I've been friends with Rafe for a while, and I never expected him to take a chance again. It was rough, the past two years, but he's finally coming back." He smiled slightly. "I'm glad he met you."

The siren stopped suddenly and the world seemed unnaturally quiet in that moment. Then the stairwell door flew open and the firemen were streaming out into the lobby. The captain was there, but no Rafe. Megan moved back near the doors with the boys, crouching with them and holding them to her side, but never taking her eyes off the exit.

Then Brad was there, held by two firefighters, his face flushed and bruised looking, his uniform torn. She hardly recognized him as the men all but dragged him past her toward police who had just come into the building. The door closed, the clang echoing, and no one else came out. Megan stared at the door, but it stayed closed. She looked up at Zane, who was talking to a policeman.

"Zane, where's Rafe?"

He turned to her. "Megan, it's—"

The door opened suddenly, and Rafe was there, stumbling forward, then righting himself. He looked around frantically, then saw the boys and her. The relief on his face was obvious as he came toward them. Megan stood when the boys pulled free and ran forward.

"Daddy! Daddy!" the twins shouted in unison, throwing themselves into his arms, hugging him as if there was no tomorrow. All Megan could do was watch the three of them.

A hand touched her shoulder. Zane. He spoke to her in a lowered voice. "He's a good man, a very good man," he said for her ears only.

Then Rafe was standing, looking at her, and Zane went toward him. "Hey, boys, how about you come home with me and play with Walker? And Anthony's over at the house, too."

Gabe hesitated, but Greg didn't. "Can we, Daddy?"

Rafe nodded, kissed each of them, then said something to Zane that Megan couldn't hear. The twins turned to her and waved. "Bye," they called, as Zane took them toward the entrance of the building.

Megan leaned back against the wall, afraid to try and stand without support. Rafe watched her as the firemen and police moved around and past him. Then he came closer, stopping within inches of her. "What...what happened?" she asked, when all she wanted to do was hold on to him and never let go.

"McMillan was taking company papers, the hard copies. Causing problems. He'd go through the trash that hadn't been shredded. All of our modern-day gadgets, and he finds out things he shouldn't by going through trash. I thought Ellen, the receptionist, was helping him, but she is just a spurned girlfriend. She quit tonight when he broke things off." Rafe laughed, a humorless sound in the almost empty area. "Tonight he tried to burn the papers, threw them into Mr. Lawrence's office and the drapes caught on fire."

"You could have been hurt," she managed to say, and hated the tears that were forming in her eyes.

He came closer, so close she could feel him exhale roughly before he spoke again. "Hey, you don't care. You told me you don't."

She hugged her arms around herself, trying to stop the trembling deep inside her. "You...made a bet with that man. To—to melt the ice princess...." Tears slipped from her eyes, but she didn't care about that now.

He touched her then, his forefinger brushing at the tears on her cheek. "How did you know that?"

"I heard you," she said, twisting away from the contact and walking as quickly as she could in the opposite direction. The first doors she saw were those to the center, and she went inside. She'd told Mary she'd talk with Rafe, but suddenly she didn't want to know anything. She didn't want to hear him say that what she'd heard was fact. She couldn't bear that.

But he was there, catching up to her near that crazy tree, and he had her by one arm, stopping her and turning her around to face him. He didn't let her go. "That's what all of that was about earlier—all that talk about last night meaning nothing? You heard me and that creep talking?"

"Yes." The word was barely audible, but it stood between them.

"Oh, Megan. Oh, damn," he said, and he pulled her to him. "It wasn't real. I was just going along with the guy to get closer to him. To figure out what he was doing and what he was up to." Rafe held her tightly, her face buried in his chest, and she could feel the rapid beating of his heart. He was as nervous as she was at that moment. "I never meant it. I never, never thought you'd overhear that. I'm so sorry."

She held on to him for support now as her legs went weak. "I heard you," she whispered.

"Well, listen to what I'm telling you," he said, his voice a rumble in his chest. He held her away and looked down into her face. "I never thought I'd say this again to anyone in my life." His hands moved to frame her face, his thumbs moving slowly on her cheeks, brushing at the tears. "I love you. I can't believe that I found you, and I'll do anything to keep you right here."

She heard the words, and for a horrifying moment,

they made no sense to her at all. Then they settled into her soul, and she understood all that she had to understand. He loved her. Mary had been right. If Megan had left, if she'd walked away from him and from the boys, she never would have known.

"Did you hear me?" he asked, his voice hoarse and slightly unsteady. "I love you, Megan Gallagher."

She reached up to touch his face, to feel the slight bristling of a new beard under her fingertips, then she skimmed her forefinger down to his throat and the pulse that beat wildly there. She felt his heart beating, and it echoed hers. Then his hand covered hers and drew it back. He looked at her bare ring finger.

"Rafe, I couldn't marry Ryan, because I love you," she whispered.

He didn't come any closer, but she felt his grasp tighten as he pulled her hand to his chest. "There's something else you need to know."

She literally stopped breathing for a moment. "What?"

"My name's Rafe, but my last name is Dagget." Now she remembered that Zane had called him that before. "Diaz is my mother's maiden name."

She didn't understand. "What?"

He held up one hand. "Just listen." She did, and when he stopped explaining she shook her head.

"You're...Dagget Security?"

"I posed as a security guard as a favor to Zane. I owe him. He was there for me when...when I needed someone. He pulled me out of a pretty deep hole." Rafe ran a hand over his face as he exhaled harshly. His wedding band was gone, but she wouldn't ask about it. Not yet. Then he framed her face again. "And you brought me back to life," he whispered roughly.

No, he'd given her life, one she'd never known before. Dagget or Diaz, a guard or a CEO? It just plain didn't matter to her, and she told him that. "I love you, whoever you are."

His touch on her stilled and his eyes grew wary. "And the boys? I know how you feel about kids, but they're part of my life. One of the best parts."

She blinked at the tears that refused to stop, going from abject misery to total joy. "Did you know that they have your dimple?" She touched the corner of his mouth with the tip of her finger. "And that look you get when you aren't sure about something, but you won't admit it? They're so much a part of you. It's a miracle."

His relief was almost tangible, and it made her smile. Really smile. That was when he drew her against him and touched her lips with his, to whisper, "When you smile at me like that...that's my miracle."

Two months later

THE MASTER BEDROOM at Rafe's house in Houston was quiet and shadowed, with soft sounds of pleasure mingling with the patter of rain on the windows.

"It's raining," Megan murmured, arching toward Rafe and his touch. "That's bad luck, to have rain on the day of a wedding."

Rafe looked down at her, his hands braced on either side of her shoulders, and marveled at them together, alone, here. "Superstition," he whispered, dipping his head to kiss her quickly. Then nothing mattered except the two of them, and the moment when they were complete. He heard a soft cry, then his own mingled with it, and he held Megan to him, rolling over, keeping her close for as long as he possibly could. She snuggled into him, making his heart lurch in the most wonderful way.

She sighed, resting her hand over his heart. "Oh, my," she said, then suddenly sat up. "Joey, the cat. He's out in the rain at the loft."

"He's okay. Zane said he got him yesterday, and he's finally staying with them," Rafe said, and pulled her back down to him. "Come on. We don't get much time alone these days, so why don't we—"

She stopped him, sitting back. "The time?"

He turned and looked at the clock by the bed. "Seven."

"Oh, no, the wedding! We're going to be late. We can't be late. I told you we shouldn't have done this."

She scrambled out of bed, stopped, went back and gave him a quick kiss, then hurried into the bathroom. "Get dressed." She looked back at him, and he saw her silhouetted naked in the doorway to the bathroom. "And no showering together. Not now." She grinned at him, then went inside.

"No showering together," he murmured, but knew that later on they would. He loved their showers. He found his suit, and by the time she came out of the bathroom, he was dressed and ready to go. He looked at her, so breathtaking in the simple white dress with its soft neckline and thin straps. She was breathtaking in or out of that dress. He held out his hand to her, and said, "Ready?"

"Oh, yes," she replied, and they hurried out of the house and through the light rain to his car.

Within ten minutes they were at the small church, running up the steps, going through the door. They looked at each other, damp but happy, and smiled, then hurried inside. The organ was already playing, and as they approached the open door to the chapel, they could see that the guests were all seated.

Zane and a very pregnant Lindsey were on the aisle with Walker. Carmella had the twins with her, and they turned to grin when they saw her and Rafe. Then the music swelled and Megan and Rafe looked down the aisle.

The front of the chapel had been draped in flowers, and a white carpet overlaid the wooden floors of the old church. The minister stood at the front, facing the guests, then spoke in a voice that carried all the way back to where Rafe and Megan hovered.

"And now, dear guests, let me present Mr. and Mrs. Robert Lewis."

Mary and Robert, the bride and groom, turned to their guests, holding hands. Mary was wearing a lovely ivory dress, Robert a perfect tuxedo that accentuated his white hair. Brittany was on one side, and Brittany's husband, Matt Terrell, on the other. Their son, Anthony, was in a tuxedo, too, standing by his father.

Megan slipped her hand into Rafe's and leaned close to her husband as the guests applauded. "I bet it was a nice wedding, but not as nice as ours,'' she whispered, then kissed his cheek.

He looked down at her, moving back from the door to make way for the bride and groom coming up the aisle. ''Ours was perfect,'' he said. It had been at the Houston house, with the boys, him and Megan, Zane and Lindsey, Mary, and a few other friends. ''Absolutely perfect.''

Megan looked up at him, and he knew that they'd only stay as long as they absolutely had to, because all bets were off when Megan smiled....

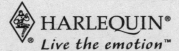

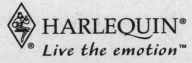

HARLEQUIN®

AMERICAN *Romance*®

proudly presents a captivating new miniseries by bestselling author

Cathy Gillen Thacker

THE BRIDES OF HOLLY SPRINGS

Weddings are serious business in the picturesque town of Holly Springs! The sumptuous Wedding Inn—the only place to go for the splashiest nuptials in this neck of the woods—is owned and operated by matriarch Helen Hart. This no-nonsense Steel Magnolia has also single-handedly raised five studly sons and one feisty daughter, so now all that's left is whipping up weddings for her beloved offspring....

Don't miss the first four installments:

THE VIRGIN'S SECRET MARRIAGE
December 2003

THE SECRET WEDDING WISH
April 2004

THE SECRET SEDUCTION
June 2004

PLAIN JANE'S SECRET LIFE
August 2004

Available at your favorite retail outlet.

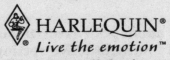

HARLEQUIN®
Live the emotion™

Visit us at www.eHarlequin.com